SILENT RUNNER
GUARDIAN WARRIOR

Creative Texts Publishers products are available at special discounts for bulk purchase for sale promotions, premiums, fund-raising, and educational needs. For details, write Creative Texts Publishers, PO Box 50, Barto, PA 19504, or visit www.creativetexts.com

SILENT RUNNT-GUARDIAN WARRIOR
by Jared McVay
Published by Creative Texts Publishers
PO Box 50
Barto, PA 19504
www.creativetexts.com

CREATESPACE EDITION

GUARDIAN WARRIOR

JARED MCVAY

To Serena

Thank you

Jared McVay

CREATIVE TEXTS PUBLISHERS

Barto, PA

This book is dedicated to all of the people searching for a little courage, love and compassion in their lives.

CHAPTER ONE

-

Black clouds rolled across the sky filling the air with thunder that sounded like a herd of large animals charging across the plains. Lightning streaked out of the clouds like shafts of death, splitting trees apart, creating fires all around her, filling the air with the smell of ozone and burning wood.

Singing Bird's lungs felt like they would burst. Her chest screamed with pain. The only reason her legs were still moving was because her brain told them to. But Singing Bird knew she couldn't run much farther. She had seen seventy-five winters and her body no longer had the strength it did when she was a young girl. In those days, she could run as fast as the wind that howled through the trees and she could outrun any of the boys in her clan. Oh, those were the glorious days, but she had no time to reminisce, danger was nipping at her heels.

As she zig-zagged between the trees, branches scraped her arms and face drawing blood that ran into her eyes, making it hard to see. The scrapes on her arms also drew blood that ran down to her hands and dripped from her fingers, leaving a trail behind her.

She glanced over her shoulder and saw the dark shadow of Father Death slowly gaining on her. From somewhere, an eerie, bone chilling voice floated through the trees, calling out to her - telling her to stop and turn around – to walk into the black cloud, telling her it was time to go to the land beyond, the place where she would be with all her friends and loved ones who had gone on before her.

Singing Bird was not afraid to die. She knew her time was near, but she was not ready to go, not yet. She still had one more thing to do and she meant to do it before she went to that place where it was always warm and you never knew hunger - the place where she and her mother would once again laugh and talk together; the place where she could gossip with her friends as they bathed in the cold water of the river, the place where the braves would eye her with desire as they had done in her youth. She would welcome death if she would be allowed to fulfill the one last thing she had promised to do.

Singing Bird's chest was heaving so hard she thought her heart would leap out of her body. The pain was getting harder to ignore. Drawing in large gulps of air, she willed her legs to keep moving, but it was getting more and more difficult and she felt herself stagger and almost go down.

As she continued to run, she prayed to the Spirit God of Mercy to grant her just a little more time, and then she would willingly and proudly go to the great beyond.

When at last her legs began to falter, she knew it was time to turn and face Father Death before she was too weak to fight; and fight she would, for she had a promise to fulfill and she would keep it, or die trying.

Singing Bird ran into a clearing no more than thirty feet across and saw a small herd of deer standing stock still, terrified by the thunder and lightning. They turned their heads and looked at her for a moment, then ran off into the forest at the other side of the clearing. It was as if they knew this was to be Singing Bird's last battleground and did not want to be near when Father Death arrived.

"I will remember you always, my beautiful friends," she said as she stopped and turned to face her fate. She knew it would make no difference but she drew her knife anyway, and held it at the ready. If she had to die, here in this clearing, she would die with the dignity of a woman of the Che-O-Wa Nation. She was, after all, the last descendant of her legendary great, great grandmother who was known by several names. In the beginning she had been called, Hummingbird. Later they called her, Silent Runner. But it was the last and final name that made Singing Bird the proudest. They called her, Guardian Warrior.

Singing Bird's body was tense, ready for the struggle. She stood up straight and stared at the approaching black cloud, wondering if there would be pain.

Suddenly, on her right, she saw the spirits of both her father and uncle with arrows notched in their bows, pointing them straight at the dark shadow coming toward her.

How could this be? she wondered. They had gone to the great beyond many winters ago during a war with the yellow haired invaders. Their names were still proudly spoken and remembered for their strength and courage.

Next, Singing Bird was startled by a deep growling on her left and when she looked in that direction, she saw her totem, the great grizzly bear standing on his hind legs with his long claws stretched toward the slow advancing shadow of death. But what startled Singing Bird the most was seeing the spirit of her mother who had now been gone ten summers. She was standing next to her totem, the great bear, holding a long spear in the throwing position, ready to defend her daughter.

Singing Bird turned her head slowly and looked behind her. She gasped when she saw the clearing was filled with the spirits of all of her old friends and relatives, all armed and ready to stand and fight for her.

Singing Bird's eyes filled with tears and she smiled, feeling their strength. She looked skyward and thanked the God of Mercy for sending the spirits to help her.

When she looked back at the advancing black cloud, she had to blink twice. Standing between her and the death shadow was a very old woman with a tattered bearskin robe draped over her stooped and bent shoulders. Her skin was brown and wrinkled and her hair was long and white. She carried no weapons, but her strength could not be denied. It radiated about her like heat from a fire on a cold night. The old woman stood without fear, facing the dark shadow of death; the same shadow that made brave warriors tremble.

The shadow slowed its forward movement as if not sure what to do.

The air crackled with tension as the death shadow came to a halt in front of the small, but powerful image blocking its way. Loud thunder rumbled across the sky; lightning bolts smashed into the ground all around them, almost knocking Singing Bird off her feet, but the old woman did not falter. She held her ground like a power that would not be denied.

Singing Bird felt the tension and wondered if the power of the old woman standing up against the death shadow would be strong enough?

Finally, the shadow of death cowered and bent to the will of the presence in front of it. The thunder and lightning ceased. The world became normal again. Then, after what seemed an eternity, the death shadow slowly began to fade back into the forest until there was nothing left but a small puff of dark smoke that drifted away into the trees.

The old woman turned in Singing Bird's direction and smiled, her eyes soft and warm. She gazed at Singing Bird with eyes that filled her with warmth and strength. There was a combination of wisdom and tiredness in her eyes that bespoke volumes about her. The old woman's lips never moved, but her hands did, deftly making the sign language she and her mother created during a time long ago when the people were still just one of the many small clans living like wild animals of the forest, stealing from one another, not trusting anyone - afraid, always afraid.

Those signs had been passed down through the ages and Singing Bird understood them as if the words had actually been spoken aloud.

Because of her mother's soft voice and the quiet way she spoke, she was called *She Who Speaks With A Soft Voice*, which translated into Clan language was simply, *Charlakavos*. The spirit of the old woman smiled and said with the silent motions of her hands moving quickly, "Your prayer has been answered. You have been given the time you asked for. Do not waste it for Father Death will not wait much longer."

Singing Bird recognized the spirit of the one whose memory she had made her promise to and her heart surged. That the spirit of her great, great grandmother would come to her in her hour of need was more than she had hoped for.

Singing Bird smiled and bowed her head in respect for her great, great grandmother; then lifted her head and watched as the spirit of the savior of the people, like the death cloud, slowly disappeared into the dark forest.

Turning her head, she noticed that as quickly as they came, the other spirits were gone and she was alone. Even though it had been late afternoon when she stopped to face Father Death, she was now standing in total darkness. The forest, the sky, the sun – all gone. There was only emptiness where there was no sight or sound.

Singing Bird stood very rigid, wondering what she was supposed to do now?

Suddenly, a reassuring voice came floating through the eerie blackness; a voice as sweet as the flowers of spring and it was calling to her.

"Singing Bird, Singing Bird. It's time. They're waiting for you."

Singing Bird felt a quiet peace settle over her and somehow knew everything would be all right. At first, she began to run slowly, then her strength returned and she ran blindly toward the voice, never worrying if she would run into something or step off into a deep chasm. She had been given the time she had prayed for. Suddenly, in the far distance, she saw a small orb of light and ran toward it.

She had gone only a short distance when she felt a soft hand touching her gently on her shoulder and suddenly, her eyes were open and she was in the light.

To her surprise, she saw the smiling face of Sparrow - Sparrow, so young and beautiful, who had recently seen her sixteenth summer, the one who would take her place when she was gone. Sparrow would be the tribe's new storyteller - keeper of the knowledge of the Che-O-Wa Nation. She had listened and remembered all the stories and she loved telling them. Singing Bird was pleased she had chosen Sparrow as her replacement. She would do well.

Singing Bird sighed with relief when she realized that everything had been a vision, a dream, and she had been granted her wish.

"It is time," Sparrow said. "They are all here, waiting for you to come and tell them the story of our humble beginnings. To tell us again of the one who breathed life into us and made us a proud people, the one who created the great Che-O-Wa Nation."

Singing Bird allowed Sparrow to help her from the place where she had been sitting leaned back against the large pecan tree, sleeping and dreaming her vision.

As the tribe's storyteller for the past fifty-nine winters, she walked proudly toward the top of the grassy knoll - her beaded dress covering her ancient and now shriveled body. Her long, white hair had been combed, hanging almost to her waist. Several hawk feathers and shiny beads had been woven into her hair for decorations and she wore the necklace that symbolized her position - a mixture of shells and stones that dated back to a time long before she had been born, during the time of her great, great grandmother.

As she labored up the knoll, strength began to surge through her body and she smiled. She had been granted her wish. She would be allowed to complete the promise she had made to the one who had created a nation to be proud of.

The hillside was filled with her people; braves of all ages, mothers with small children. Everyone was there, waiting for her. Sitting directly in front of where she stood, sat the great chief, Big Nose and his council of braves. Big Nose nodded and smiled.

When Singing Bird saw that even the children were looking up at her, waiting to hear the story, she knew all was as it should be. The old ways would live on through the children and their humble beginnings would never be forgotten.

Sparrow would keep up the tradition of gathering the young ones around her and telling the stories of their past. Singing Bird rejoiced in the fact that Sparrow was proud to have been the one chosen to replace her, and would do her best to live up to the tradition.

Singing Bird reached the crest of the small hill and looked out over the wide valley, her heart swelling with joy. No longer did they live like wild animals, nor were they afraid of anyone. The only time there was war was when someone, like the Yellow Hairs, tried to invade them and tried to take them as slaves or steal their property as they had in the far distant past – but no longer. Over the years they had become a strong people; good people who enjoyed life and what Mother Nature provided for them, always sharing love and laughter instead of fear and war.

Singing Bird raised her hands for quiet. Even the dogs dropped down on their stomachs and looked at her as though they too wanted to hear her story.

CHAPTER TWO

-

Singing Bird stood for a long moment, capturing the faces of her people one last time. She knew her time was near as the vision had told her, and shortly after fulfilling her promise, she would go to meet her friends and relatives in the great beyond and she was no longer afraid.

Singing Bird looked to her left and saw Squirrel, the new tribal historian, sitting next to a large piece of wood, using it like a table. On top, were the things Squirrel would need to record the story so it would never be forgotten. There were seven writing quills, a pot of ink made from charcoal, and a stack of soft pieces of doeskin to write on.

Telling the story of her great, great grandmother one last time was the promise she had made to her, only this time it would be put down in writing for all generations to know of their humble beginnings.

Never before had any of the stories been written down; only passed from storyteller to storyteller. But this story, the most cherished of all their stories, needed to be written down so it would never be forgotten or miss-told by those following her.

Being the tribal storyteller for almost her entire lifetime, and last surviving descendant of the legendary, Silent Runner-Guardian Warrior, it was Singing Bird's honor to be the one to tell the story so it could be written down, as only she could tell it.

Squirrel smiled and nodded her head, indicating she was ready.

Singing Bird turned back and looked out across the crowd of faces. The moon had just come over the horizon and was full and shone down on the people who looked back at her. She stepped out onto a large piece of rock jutting out from the knoll, like a small stage.

"Brothers and Sisters. I come before you to fulfill a promise I made to the memory of the one who pulled us from darkness and showed us the light – the one who made us who we are today, the people of the mighty Che-O-Wa Nation."

There was great cheering until Singing Bird raised her hands for silence.

"Many, many moons ago, during a time before time as we now know it, there was a great time of darkness, a time before we were a people. We roamed these mountains in small clans, living like animals – afraid of the other clans who also moved from place to place as we did. We were even afraid of each other. We had no destination, no dreams but to survive from one day to the next. We raided the other clans and stole women and small children, then traded them for food to fill our bellies and skins to keep out the cold when we could not provide for ourselves, as did they to us. We knew nothing. We had no weapons other than the rocks from the ground or pieces of wood to be used like clubs. Nor did we understand how to govern ourselves. We spoke mainly with grunts. Except for their brute strength, our leaders were not strong. Their minds were closed and their beliefs were false beliefs - like believing if a crow landed near you, death would be only a short distance behind it. Oh, how foolish were our beliefs in those days."

Singing Bird looked at Sparrow and nodded toward the water skin laying next to her.

Sparrow brought the skin filled with cold water recently taken from the nearby stream. Singing Bird took her time, allowing the cool water to relieve her parched throat.

During this time, two braves carried a large piece of log up the hill and stood it behind where Singing Bird was standing so she would have something to sit on while telling her story. It was tall enough so she could still see out over her people and they could see her. One of the braves placed a soft piece of bearskin on top of the log so it would be more comfortable for Singing Bird to sit on, should she get tired of standing.

The people remained silent and waited. Singing Bird had grown old and they would honor her by waiting until she was ready to continue.

The cool water gave her strength and she felt renewed energy. She eased herself onto the log and smiled.

"During this time long ago, a middle-aged woman who was known as *She Who Speaks With A Soft Voice*, or *Charlakavos*, suffered much pain as she brought new life into the world in the form of a small girl child and when the women who had assisted in the birthing saw the baby was alive, one of them wrapped the small child in a piece of soft skin and handed the infant to Charlakavos, who thought that the age of forty-nine summers, was too old to be having a child. No other woman in the clan had ever given birth at that age. But she had, and would be looked down upon, or greatly respected - she wasn't yet sure which.

"Charlakavos held her daughter in her arms and marveled at the child's beauty. She had two strong sons, but neither one compared to the beauty of her newborn child. Looking down at her daughter, Charlakavos knew the elders would not be happy, but the gods had spoken and she had born a girl child.

"She whispered - your skin is lighter than my skin. And your eyes and hair are the color of your father, who was one of the Yellow Hairs that raided us, but your smile and your beauty are like mine. I am sorry my child, but because you are a female, you will have a hard life. But know this, I will always be there for you."

Singing Bird took a breath and saw the nodding heads as they became enveloped in the story. And for many of the young ones, this would be the first time they heard of their beginnings and were staring at her, wide eyed, as she continued.

"The elders of the clan stood outside the hut, anxiously waiting for the arrival of new life. If it was a boy, the parents would be revered, for males were needed to help with the hunting and the raids when they got older. But, if the gods were angered and it was a female, the father would be looked down upon as not being strong enough to produce a male heir and would lose status in the clan. A female child would be considered a burden – just another mouth to feed. Except for breeding and taking care of the men, women were considered useless for they could never be warriors; they were believed to be too weak.

"They awaited the boisterous sound of a male child's wailing cry that always came shortly after being born, but none came and they were confused and scared. Was something wrong? Why hadn't the child made any sounds?

"Inside the hut, Charlakavos noticed the baby's silence, but she was too carried away by her new daughter's beauty, and the fact that she was alive, to worry about it. She would make noises when she felt like it, and not before. Many years ago, when she was younger, she had lost two female babies during the birthing, and wanted desperately for this one to live, even though she and the child would be looked down on for more reasons than was normal.

"The women who had assisted Charlakavos with her birthing had noticed the baby's silence, and they were afraid. It was not normal, even for a female child, not to cry shortly after being born. They looked at each other, not sure what to do."

'And how will you be called?' "Charlakavos asked looking down at the child cradled in her arms, never realizing the answer to her question would become known to her very shortly, and in a way she never expected."

Singing Bird stopped again and rubbed her upper arms. The night air was cool and she was beginning to get slightly chilled.

Immediately, Sparrow rushed up and draped a fur-lined skin over her shoulders.

Singing Bird tugged the skin around her and smiled at Sparrow. "Thank you," she said, and then took a sip of water before beginning, again.

"Charlakavos had barely posed the question of what to name her newborn child, when out of nowhere, there came a fluttering noise at the opening of the hut. The women looked in that direction and to their surprise, hovering in the opening was a small, female hummingbird.

"The people standing outside saw the tiny, green feathered bird dart out of the forest and come to the opening of the hut and hover there. The people all stepped back, some drawing loud breaths. They were both, puzzled and afraid. Why would a hummingbird be looking into the hut, they wondered - was this a sign? Yes, they thought. It was a sign, but what the sign meant, they had no idea and mutterings began amongst them.

"Standing there, mesmerized, they watched with amazement and more gasps when the small bird darted inside the hut.

"The women inside the hut stepped back in fear as the small bird flew directly over to Charlakavos and her newborn daughter and hovered in front of them, its little wings moving faster than their eyes could see. Then it darted back and forth in front of the newborn child, its tiny wings making fluttering sounds, while from its throat came a high-pitched noise that sounded like a cricket rubbing its back legs together.

"The little hummingbird flitted back and forth as if it was making a fuss over the new born child; then stopped suddenly in front of the child for just a moment before turning and darting out through the opening of the hut and disappearing back into the forest.

"Charlakavos smiled. She had been sent a sign. Although she didn't quite understand what the sign meant, she knew in her heart, it had been a sign. Unlike the other people of the clan, she believed the sign to be a good one, but she would need the council of her husband and possibly their chief, or even the medicine man.

"Taking her child in her arms, Charlakavos went to seek the wisdom of her husband, He Who Fishes. He Who Fishes had been named so because he was the best fisherman in the clan and held status in the chief's council.

"He Who Fishes was a proud man who loved his wife even though she had been taken captive by the Yellow Hairs during a raid some ten moons ago. After having been raped and beaten, she escaped; wandering back into the clan, dirty, ragged, and half starved.

As far as he knew, he and his wife, Charlakavos, were the only ones to know about her being raped and who the real father of the child was, although there had been whispers when she announced she was with child."

Singing Bird looked out across the valley where people sat in silence, awaiting her next words. The valley was a good one because she could whisper and it would be heard clear over on the far side – the rock formations made it a natural amphitheater, allowing the speaker to speak as they normally did, which allowed Singing Bird to tell this lengthy story without hurting her throat. After a moment, she continued.

"When He Who Fishes looked down at the child and saw that it was a female child, his heart sank. The clan would ridicule him for not being strong enough to create a male child, and he would have to suffer in silence, for he hadn't sired the child. If the truth became known, Charlakavos would be banished from the clan and he would lose even more status, possibly also being banished for hiding the truth.

"He Who Fishes continued to work on the fishing net he was repairing while he listened to the story of the hummingbird; and when his wife finished, He Who Fishes laid down his tools and stared at the sky for a long while. He did not want to be involved with trying to interpret this sign for several reasons. First, the child was not his; and second, it was a female child and not worthy of his attention; and third, he was not good at interpreting signs.

"Finally, he looked down at Charlakavos and the child she held in her arms and said," 'Come, we will seek the wisdom of Owl,' "a slight smile crossing his lips for taking himself out of the decision making.

"Owl had been the clan's medicine man for as long as He Who Fishes could remember. He was considered wise and his medicine strong. When he was but sixteen summers, he provided a cure for the chief's aching teeth. The clan marveled at this and named him Owl because owls were believed to be wise and this young man was wise beyond his age.

"Two moons later, the old medicine man who was called Quiet One because he rarely spoke, passed on to the next world after being bitten by a snake that rattled its tail.

"As was their custom in those days, a great pile of brush and wood was made and the body was placed on top, then the brush was set on fire. The whole clan would stand and watch as the smoke carried the person's soul to the great beyond.

"And on the rare occasion when the smoke drifted off into the forest instead of rising into the sky, they believed this to be a sign that this person was not worthy of going to the great beyond and was destined to wander the forest forever as a lost soul. From that point on, their name would be stricken from their memories so as not to bring bad luck on themselves, or to the clan.

"Even as old as he now was, Owl still stood tall and slender, his wizened face a mass of wrinkles. But it was his eyes that showed his strength for they were still bright and dark brown. He could make a person believe he was staring into their very soul.

"After listening to Charlakavos's story, Owl lit his pipe and smoked for what seemed to be a long time. Finally, he looked at the child, knowingly. He said nothing of what he thought about who the real father was – that would come in time when the knowledge needed to come out, but for now, he would do as his duty as medicine man dictated."

'Yes, I believe you have had a sign, and now you want me to tell you what it means,' "Owl said, nodding his head thoughtfully.

"He Who Fishes had seen something in Owl's eyes as he

stared down at the child, and knew the wise old medicine man understood the truth about the newborn in front of him. But how did he know? he wondered. They had told no one. Then he nodded his head slightly, he was after all, Owl, knower of secrets.

"Charlakavos also saw the look in the medicine man's eyes and felt a catch in her breath."

'Yes,' "she said to Owl, wondering if she should reveal the truth about her child, which would mean banishment, or worse, both her and her child would be stoned to death. After a moment of thought, she decided to wait and see what the future held."

Singing Bird stopped her storytelling, again, and took another sip of water from the skin and watched as the moon began its ascent above the tops of the trees. The moon was large tonight, and would be bright and full, filling the valley with its warm light. She also noticed that torches were being lit in various places around the area, adding extra light, but very little heat. The cooking fires would provide whatever heat that would be needed when it got cooler, as it did at night here in the mountains.

The story of their beginnings was a long one – the longest of any of her stories, but it was also the story most cherished by everyone.

Looking upward once again, Singing Bird noticed the night sky had somehow become filled with twinkling stars and she wondered if any of those stars were giant pieces of land and water like this place where she and the others lived? Could there be life out there? And were they people or just bans of small clans like her people used to be? Life was indeed a mystery, but she had no time to sit around pondering on the mysteries of it all, she had a story to tell.

Singing Bird took a deep breath and began again. "Charlakavos was worried her secret would become known, which would not only bring shame to her husband, but she and her baby would be turned out. How would they survive out in the forest, alone, with no way to protect herself and her child from the wild animals, or the cruelty of Mother Nature? She had known of several small children who had been born with some sort of deformity and had been taken into the forest and left - only to be carried off by bears and cougars or other large animals, which caused her to shudder.

"Charlakavos suddenly felt very nervous as Owl walked over and stared down at the newborn child for what seemed a long time. She could feel her legs getting weak and her heart beginning to pound.

"Finally, he looked directly into her eyes and said," 'This is indeed an interesting story. I am having several thoughts about its meaning and feel the need to council with our chief, Sleeps and Thinks.'

"And with that, Owl walked out of his hut, searching for Sleeps and Thinks.

"Charlakavos let out a sigh of relief. He had said nothing about the child being different with its light skin and yellow hair. As she trailed after him, she could only hope she and her child would be allowed to remain among the clan, where, even though life would be hard, at least they would be somewhat safe.

"He Who Fishes followed along, wondering how it would end. He had seen the look in the medicine man's eyes. Would he reveal his thoughts to the chief? And what about himself, would he be turned out, too? He was not the strong man he pretended to be. Where would he go? How would he survive?

"Their chief - Sleeps and Thinks was originally known as Great Bear, back during his younger years because of his giant size and temperament. If anyone came near when he was resting, he would growl at them. And when faced with an enemy, he would growl loudly as he charged into battle. He was a strong fighter and warriors from the other clans were afraid of him, for he had never been bested. His body was heavily scarred from past battles and he had a story to go with each scar, which he loved to tell about.

"After making him chief, the people changed his name to Sleeps and Thinks because anytime they went to council with him, they found him asleep and upon waking him, they were told he hadn't been asleep at all, but thinking.

"No one had argued with him, but all snickered under their breath because no one snored as loud as he did just from thinking.

"So, when Owl, Charlakavos and He Who Fishes approached their chief, they found him down next to the river, reclining against a tree, thinking and snoring loudly."

'It looks as though our leader is in deep thought about the problems of his people,' "Owl said over his shoulder.

"Both, Charlakavos and He Who Fishes had to put their hands over their mouths to hold back the laughter they felt."

At this, there were chuckles from the people sitting on the grassy valley, and especially the children, who laughed out loud with the thought of the ancient chief snoring loudly as each one envisioned their fathers at times, while sitting along a riverbank, sleeping instead of fishing as they were supposed to be doing.

Singing Bird smiled and reached for the water skin, glad she was able to sit down. At her age, standing for long periods of time was very tiring and caused her knees and feet to hurt. Just knowing this would be the last time she told the story gave her strength to carry on, and when the laughter died down, she continued.

"After gently awakening their chief, Owl explained why they were there and Sleeps and Thinks agreed to listen to Charlakavos's tale of the hummingbird.

"When she finished, the chief stood up and stretched, then walked along the riverbank with his hands behind his back, as though he was in deep thought, leaving Owl, Charlakavos and He Who Fishes, waiting for his answer.

"Finally, Sleeps and Thinks stopped and moved his long, black hair to the side so he could scratch the back of his neck; and when he finished, he turned to them and said in a voice that sounded like it was coming from the back of a deep cave."

'That was an interesting story, yes, very interesting indeed. This is a story that will take meditating on to find the answer to its true meaning. Yes, I will meditate and have an answer for you tomorrow,' "and with that, the chief walked over and sat down next to the tree – leaned against it and closed his eyes.

"As they walked away, the old chief opened one eye just enough to watch them leave.

"He had seen the blue eyes of the baby, along with the lightness of her skin, which told him the answer to the question in everyone's mind since the day Charlakavos had announced she was going to bring new life into their clan. There was no doubt in his mind the child would be marked as a Yellow Hair, which meant he would have to banish them both. He Who Fishes would also have to be banished for keeping the secret. This saddened his heart for he liked them both, and hated to lose He Who Fishes. Sometimes being a chief was not good.

"The following morning Sleeps and Thinks called the entire clan together, instructing them to sit close to the large fire in the center of their village - and when they were all seated, he began."

'As you all know, we have a newborn child among us – a girl child, born yesterday to He Who Fishes and Charlakavos. We were all hoping for a male child, but it seems the gods have turned their backs on us. Maybe they know something we have yet to learn,' "he said, cautiously.

"Sleeps and Thinks was trying to choose his words carefully, for if he was wrong in what he said and did, he would look bad, but if his thinking was correct, he would be honored for his insight and could do what was expected of him, which was not to his liking, but knew he would do what their laws demanded, because that's what chiefs did."

'Shortly after the birthing of the child, an incident happened that I believe was a sign,' "he told them." 'But, before giving my interpretation of what the sign means, and what to do about it, I will have Charlakavos, tell you in her own words, what happened.'

"Holding her child close to her, Charlakavos stood up and faced the people of her clan, who stared back with hostility on their faces. Several of them glared at her menacingly, causing her to cringe. Drawing on all of her courage, she met their gaze and began.

"After telling the story of the small hummingbird entering the hut and fussing around her and her newborn child, Charlakavos told them she had decided it had been a sign to name her daughter, Hummingbird, nothing more and nothing less. She could only hope they would believe her.

"From the back, a tall, muscular brave stood up, placing his arms across his chest. He was one of the people whose eyes showed hostility. As a warrior with many triumphs against the other clans, he held much status. He was powerful in more ways than just raiding other clans; there was a cunning and cruelty about him that the clan members feared, and when he spoke, they listened.

"When Charlakavos saw who it was, a lump formed in her throat and a knot grew in her stomach. It was Hawk, and he was still angry because all those many seasons ago, he had wanted her for his mate, but instead, she had chosen He Who Fishes. And now, Hawk was about to get his revenge. She could hear it in his voice and see it in his eyes."

'What do we care what she names the whelp? The brat has not made a sound since it was born because it is cursed! Yes, cursed!

Look at it with its light skin, blue eyes and yellow hair! It is not of our blood, but the blood of the Yellow Hair Charlakavos laid with during her absence. I say Charlakavos has been cursed by the gods for what she did, and has given her this deformed whelp as a damnation upon her,' "Hawk said in a, loud, clear voice.

"Immediately, there were murmurs bouncing off the tongues of the people; some of them nodding their heads in agreement.

"Sleeps and Thinks lowered his head so they would not see the smile that crossed his face. He would not have to make a decision about what to do, Hawk had done it for him, and the people would demand he follow their code and banish them both.

"Charlakavos started to say something in her defense, but Hawk raised his hand and halted her."

'Let her deny that the whelp's father is a Yellow Hair. Look at it! It does not look like any one of us! I say she went willingly with the Yellow Hairs and when she tired of them, came sneaking back, believing we would not realize what she had been up to.'

"Again, shouts of agreement could be heard, as Hawk looked around, seeing the anger on their faces, knowing he had put Charlakavos in a bad position with the rest of the clan."

Singing Bird shuddered; feeling the pain and anguish Charlakavos must have felt at that moment.

"Hawk was far from being finished as he shouted," 'If we allow this adulteress who has betrayed her own people and mingled with our enemy, the Yellow Hairs, to stay among us with her cursed and deformed offspring, then the gods will surely frown down on us and we will be doomed! Who agrees with me? Short of stoning, banishment is the only answer!'

"Hawk's voice rose to a high pitch, which sent the people into a frenzy. Several of them were so worked up they threw rocks at Charlakavos and her baby. One of the rocks struck Charlakavos a glancing blow to the head as she turned, holding her baby close to her, trying to protect her child, as blood ran down into her eye."

'And her husband, He Who Fishes, knew about this all along and did nothing,' "Hawk declared, waving his arms widely about him.

"He had their attention and was in control, turning them into a crazed, fearful mob. His next statement, he hoped, would also rid the clan of the man who stole Charlakavos from him all those many moons ago."

'I say He Who Fishes should also be banished, for he is no longer a man! He is a coward who allows his mate to lay with our enemy!'

"Shouts rose from the people and they began to shout," 'Leave! Banishment to all of them! Kill them for they will bring a curse down upon us! Banishment, banishment!'

"Charlakavos turned and looked for her husband, hoping for some protection and guidance about what to do, but he was nowhere to be seen. Like a coward he had sneaked away when Hawk spoke his name. He had always been a kind and gentle man, but never had she thought of him as a coward, until now. At this point, she looked toward Sleeps and Thinks as he stood up, raising up both arms, motioning for them to quiet down. He was her last hope.

"When they finally quieted down, the chief turned and stared at Charlakavos before declaring," 'By your actions, you have been found guilty of bringing a curse down upon us and by our laws, you, your whelp and your mate, He Who Fishes, are banished from our clan. Your names will be stricken from our tongues and your images will be erased from our memories. You have until the sun reaches its highest point to be gone. If you are still here when that time comes, you and your damnation will be stoned to death. It is the law and I have spoken. Now go before I change my mind and kill you myself to appease the gods for what you have done.'

"By now, Hawk had come from the back of the crowd and stood next to Sleeps and Thinks and slapped him on the back, acknowledging he had done the right thing. He had been given his revenge. His next quest would be to get rid of Sleeps and Thinks and become the new leader of the clan. It would be only a matter of time for he had a plan.

"Hawk watched, with a broad smile on his face, as Charlakavos staggered with a heavy heart toward her hut. She would gather her few belongings and leave their clan, forever, taking the brat with her. He Who Fishes had run away like the coward he had always been, which meant Charlakavos and her whelp would be easy prey for the animals of the forest. He had been patient, and now revenge for what she did to him was his, and he was pleased.

"Unbeknownst to the others, Little Otter, who was

Charlakavos's best friend, had sneaked away and was waiting in her hut when Charlakavos entered. For a moment, Charlakavos was startled and only relaxed when she saw Little Otter smile and hold out the bundle of food."

'I am so sorry. I will miss you. I do not feel as the others do. I know you did not willingly do as Hawk suggested. For during their raid, they did the same thing to me, only the gods did not see fit to burden me with a child, nor did the Yellow Hairs take me captive, for I am not pretty like you,' "Little Otter, said, lowering her eyes.

"Charlakavos was shocked to learn what had happened to Little Otter, and felt an even stronger bond between them but said nothing about her looks."

'I will try from time to time to sneak away and bring you what I can, but it will be difficult, for if anyone finds out...' "Little Otter said, hanging her head in shame for her weakness.

"Charlakavos laid her hand on Little Otter's arm and said, with tears streaming down her face," 'It is alright. We may be far away and hard to find, but you will always be in my heart for we are now truly sisters. If you cannot come, I will understand that, also. Do not put yourself in danger or feel obligated, and do not feel shame. You were taken by force, just as I was.'

"After they hugged, Little Otter looked down at the baby and said," 'I, too, believe it was a sign and I agree, you should call her, Hummingbird.'

"Little Otter placed a kiss on Hummingbird's forehead, then went out through the back opening of the hut and quickly disappeared.

"Charlakavos stood for a moment, sorrow engulfing her. She was alone, and to survive in the forest with the wild animals seeking an easy prey, she would need to remember all her mother and father had taught her. It had not been her fault the Yellow Hairs had taken her. Nor had she given in willingly - they had held her down. But she hadn't been allowed to tell her side of it. Hawk was a strong voice in the clan and being a woman, she could not stand against him. Even her husband had been afraid of Hawk and had deserted her.

"She did not understand why the gods had allowed this to happen, but she knew they had their reasons, for they did not do things without having a plan. What their plan was for her and her child, she did not know. Only with patience would their plan be revealed to her. She was not ashamed of her beautiful child and would do everything in her power to see her daughter grow into womanhood. Maybe she would find a mate among another clan, but that was highly unlikely. Who would want a woman with a child who looked like their enemy? She was glad her parents had gone to the great beyond and had not been here to witness her shame."

CHAPTER THREE

-

Singing Bird took a deep breath and exhaled slowly. The telling of the story was an emotional one for her, but after a moment, she was able to continue.

"From a safe distance, Charlakavos stood looking back down the mountainside at the only home she'd ever known. Tears streamed down her face. She and her baby were alone. The people she'd grown up with had turned against her with their foolish beliefs and her husband, He Who Fishes, the man who had promised to take care of her, had deserted her, sneaking off and disappearing like a rat seeking a place to hide.

"After taking another deep breath, she turned away from the ones who stood staring back at her, some with rocks or clubs in their hands.

"Without a word, she hoisted the pack on her back into a more comfortable position and then settled Hummingbird, as she was now called, into her place in the cradle hanging down the front of her, and headed up the mountainside. The forest was thick and the trees overlapped each other, blocking out most of the sun, allowing only slivers of light to stream through small openings in their search for the ground.

"The first thing she would need to do, Charlakavos thought, was to find shelter. At the height she would be going to, the nights would be cold and there was always the possibility of storms. Watching as she struggled up the mountain, she hoped she would be able to find enough downfall limbs to make a lean-to of sorts, at least for the time being, until she could find a permanent location to make her home, far away from the clan. To stay too close would be like inviting the young bucks of the clan to come sniffing around with lust on their minds, since she would now be fair game as were the females of other clans.

"That night she sat beneath a quickly thrown together shelter made of fallen limbs and brush. Her fire was small and fortunately, even though the weather grew cold, it did not rain.

"Sitting next to the small fire with her newborn child in her arms, she looked into the baby's eyes and realized the child was staring back at her."

'Somehow, some way, we will survive and we will show them all that you are not wicked, or cursed, but someone special. You are born of two worlds which makes you very special, indeed.'

"Hummingbird looked up at her mother as though she understood each and every word, but made no sound, not even a whimpering noise.

"For Charlakavos, the following weeks were tedious. She had to draw on her memory and bring to mind the things she had only half heartily taken notice of as a child. Fortunately, she had listened more than she realized when her mother and grandmother had taught her about the edibles and medicines to be found in the forest. And by pure luck and a good throwing arm, she killed several rabbits, and once, a high mountain grouse, by throwing rocks at them as they sat quietly, hoping she would not see them.

"At first, she was scared when the visions came in her dreams about things she would need to survive, such as weapons to not only protect herself and her child, but also to bring down large game. No one had ever used anything but clubs and rocks, so the thought of making the strange bent piece of wood with a long piece of hide between the ends that would shoot a long shaft with a piece of pointed rock on the end of it caused her to question her sanity. They were things she remembered seeing when she had been among the Yellow Hairs. They had them and used them to bring down game or overpower anyone who stood in their way. She had asked the gods to help her and here was evidence, strange as it was, that they were answering her prayers. Maybe she and her child had not been cursed, but turned out for another reason. What that was, she had no idea, but why else would she have the visions? Somehow, they must survive.

"On rainy days when she could not hunt, and by the firelight in the evenings, she made a stone axe with a strong handle that she wore at her waist, a small knife made from a piece of flint rock that fit into the palm of her hand to skin the animals with, a strong bow and a quiver filled with arrows, along with several animal traps, and a hunting knife that had a bone handle and the blade was made from a long, slender piece of stone that she sharpened to a point at the end

– and last, a spear made from a long, slender piece of tree limb, with a piece of pointed rock bound to one end; all, things from her visions. It took practice but soon she was able to use each weapon with a certain amount of skill.

"The small animals she was able to bring down, provided her with the nourishment she needed, and their skins were made into moccasins of a sort for her feet, and clothing for Hummingbird. They were not the same as she'd learned to make when she was with the clan for she did not have time to cure the skins properly. She needed coverings for her feet, and clothes for her child and she needed them, now. She would make proper foot wear and clothes at a later time, after she found a place to make a home and prepare for the cold weather which she knew would be upon them soon.

"Her biggest prize so far was the small bear she'd brought down with her bow and arrows. It had been a close call. They had almost bumped into each other while she was searching for food. She was busy looking for berries and not paying attention to the warning signs around her. Her eyes had been staring at the ground when she heard the growl. When she looked up, there it was, standing on its hind legs, growling, its teeth bared, with its deadly claws pointed at her.

"Instinct told her to run, but common sense said that would be useless since bears could run faster than people. Plus, she was carrying her child in a pouch on her back. Drawing on all of her courage, she took her bow from where it hung on her shoulder, then notched an arrow and drew back the string made from a long piece of skin. She took a deep breath and hoped her aim would be true.

"Just as she released the arrow, the bear dropped down to all four feet and the arrow embedded itself in the bear's neck, not in its heart as she'd hoped for. The bear growled and swatted at the arrow sticking out of its neck, breaking off the shaft, leaving only the embedded arrowhead.

"By that time, Charlakavos had notched a second arrow and when the bear stood up again, she let the arrow fly. This time it drove itself straight into the bear's heart.

"He stood there for a moment, as if he was confused; then like a tree being felled, he toppled over, driving the arrowhead deeper into his chest.

"Charlakavos stayed a safe distance until she was sure the bear was dead, and even then, she approached it with caution. Before taking her skinning knife from the pouch at her waist, she thanked the gods for providing for her. This would not only give her a great deal of meat, but also fat for cooking and a warm cover for the cold nights. There would be nothing wasted. Even the claws and bones would be made useful.

"Each day, she climbed higher up the mountain, taking her time, seeking game, water, and always on the lookout for a place to build a hut.

"Four moons had passed when by chance, Charlakavos, while out checking one of her traps, happened to notice what might be an opening in the mountainside, a shadow, hidden behind some large boulders and several bushes.

"After tearing the bushes away, she stared into the entrance of what looked to be a very large cave and she felt her heart begin to pound with excitement. Could this be what she'd been looking for? She turned and looked in all directions and all she could see was forest. She looked at the sky, felt the coolness of the air and knew she was high on the mountain, far away from the clan that had turned her out. Up here, she would see no one from any of the clans for they were afraid to go too far from their camp because of their fear of the large animals or possibly running into the Yellow Hairs.

"The sun shone brightly down on the small, secluded area, like a sign. It was high up, near the top of the mountain and Charlakavos had a wide field of view. Below her, the trees stood tall and proud as far as she could see. Large boulders were scattered in front of the cave opening like a barrier wall, concealing the entrance. Even she had almost missed seeing it, which would be to her advantage if either, two or four legged predators came prowling around. This would be a good place, she decided. Here, she would make a home for herself and Hummingbird – her only hope was that the cave would be habitable, which still remained to be seen.

"Since there had been a large bush standing at the entrance to the cave, there was little chance any large animals would be making their home there, and any small ones that might be inside would wind up in a stew. Although she didn't know it, there would be no snakes at this high altitude, but it was one of the things she looked for.

"Looking around, she saw downfall, giving her a source of fuel for cooking and heating the cave. There would be game if she hunted on the other side of the mountain, for she was sure once she and Hummingbird moved into the cave, all the large animals would move away because of their natural fear of humans.

"Inside the cave, Charlakavos was amazed at its size. The cave was at least twice the size of the hut she'd lived in when she was with the clan, and deep inside, there was running water that flowed out of a crack in the rock into a small pool that never seemed to fill up or overflow. Where the water went, she had no idea, but having water inside the cave was a great advantage. Should anyone come snooping around, she could hide in here indefinitely, or as long as her food supply lasted. With a little planning, and luck, she and Hummingbird would be safe. Plus, she had weapons to defend herself and Hummingbird with that none of the others had ever seen, which due to their beliefs would cause them to think she was in league with the mountain devils.

"There was no fear of a night attack because of the soul takers. The clan believed the soul takers were evil spirits that roamed the woods at night, searching for anyone who happened to come within their grasp, and for that reason, they kept large fires going all night inside their huts and in the common area outside. No one left the area after the sun went down. But by now, after being alone in the forest for all these many moons, Charlakavos was coming to realize the old beliefs were nothing more than fearful tales someone had conjured up in their minds, and during storytelling times had convinced the others the stories were true.

"This information, along with all the skills she was learning, she would pass on to her daughter so she would not grow up, fearful of unseen spirits or devils. She would teach Hummingbird to think for herself and only believe what she could prove to be true.

"The area in front of the cave was a wide, solid rock ledge, so she wouldn't leave tracks coming and going, and the downfall in the forest would hide her footsteps, especially with the soft fur shoes she would make that were pliable and left hardly any evidence of her passing. With time and some hard work, she could make a comfortable home here for herself and her daughter.

"Once again, she looked at the sky and gave thanks to the gods for leading her here. She hugged Hummingbird close to her and said," 'We have a home, little one. We have a home. The gods have not forsaken us, as the people down below believe they would. They have led us here for a reason. I do not know yet what the reason is, but I am sure they will tell us when the time is right.'

CHAPTER FOUR

-

Singing Bird's eyes had been closed; envisioning the cave and the happiness Charlakavos would have in her new home. She had told the story many times in the past, and always got the same reaction at this part of the telling. When she felt a soft hand touch her on her shoulder, she jumped slightly. After a moment, she opened her eyes slowly, not wanting to lose the happy feeling, and saw the lovely face of Sparrow standing next to her.

'It is time to take a break in the storytelling and eat something' "Sparrow said." 'Moon Glow and several others have prepared food for you.'

Singing Bird looked out over the people and saw small fires burning and could smell the wonderful aromas floating through the air, gracing her nose and felt her stomach growl. She watched as Moon Glow, a long and dear friend stood up and motioned for her to come down to her fire.

Sparrow helped her to stand, and walked with her down the hill to Moon Glow's fire, where more food awaited her than she could possibly eat.

After stuffing herself with fresh cooked meat, wild berries, and a drink Moon Glow had made from various herbs and spices, Sparrow accompanied her back up the hill to her stool, and when she was comfortable, she resumed the story of their beginnings, for there was still much to tell.

Once again, Singing Bird looked out across the valley and saw faces staring back at her, waiting for her to begin, again.

"For several long days, Charlakavos worked tirelessly to turn the cave into a home for herself and Hummingbird. Toward the back of the cave, where it was dry, she stacked enough firewood to last several moons. There were large pieces that would last the night, and there were smaller pieces to be used to get a good flame going. With brush and limbs, she made a covering for the entrance of the cave. It would not only hide the opening, but also keep out the cold weather when it came. She found a hollow place back from the opening that she could use as a fire pit. It would not only be a good place to cook their food, but far enough inside to warm the entire cave. At first, Charlakavos was concerned about the smoke from the fire filling the cave with the entrance covered, but once she had a fire going, she noticed that it did not fill the cave, nor did it seek the opening where it would be sucked out into the forest, but rose and disappeared into cracks in the ceiling. Where it went, she did not know, but at least no one would see it coming from the entrance of the cave if they happened to be in the vicinity. She smiled. Here was yet another reason to feel happy about their new home. The gods were surely looking out for her.

"During all the moons since Hummingbird's birth, she had

still not uttered a sound. She was growing like a weed and was crawling around, getting into things, and even trying to stand. When Charlakavos would scold her, she would look at her mother as though she understood every word. Her eyes were keen and took in everything, and her hearing was like that of an animal. She could hear sounds long before her mother could, and she was strong and healthy in every way. Except for not being able to make sounds, she was perfect. Her eyes were now a steel blue that highlighted her long, blonde hair, and her light skin was now tanned from being out in the sun. She seemed to be growing on a daily basis, and Charlakavos could see she would someday become a beautiful young lady. She would be tall and slender, like her father, who even though he had been her abductor and sworn enemy, Charlakavos had to admit, he had been a fine man to look at – and brave, for the others looked up to and seemed to respect him.

"It was Hummingbird who initiated the sign language that was to become a way to communicate with each other. She had just passed eleven moons and was walking around with ease, even running when she got the chance. Charlakavos was kneeling next to the fire, checking the meat that was roasting on the stick when Hummingbird raced up next to her and stopped. Charlakavos looked up at her daughter and got a look of shock on her face. Hummingbird was making a motion with her hands, pointing toward her mouth and rubbing her stomach, indicating she was hungry.

"Charlakavos stared at Hummingbird for what seemed to be a long time, trying to understand what she'd just seen. Untrained, her daughter was trying to talk to her with a new way of speaking. Charlakavos was thinking about how to make signs with her hands that would tell her daughter that it would be another few minutes when Hummingbird indicated her mouth with one hand and with the other made the sign of talking, then pointed to her mother with one hand and pointed to her ear with the other, nodding her head up and down.

"She was indicating she could hear and understand the spoken word! The gods had truly blessed her with intelligence. Someday, the clan would regret turning them out. Of this, she had no doubt. Two days later, Hummingbird heard someone near the cave and alerted her mother, and to their delight it was Little Otter searching for them. She would have walked right past the cave had not Hummingbird heard her. Little Otter was in awe of the cave and all that had been done, and swore to return as often as she could.

"Charlakavos stood at the entrance of the cave, looking out at the sky, watching as snow began to cling to the trees and cover the ground. She smiled as Hummingbird walked up and stood next to her. They would be safe during the time of heavy snow and cold weather. She had worked long hard days, with Hummingbird helping as much as she could and they were ready. She had enough wood piled inside to see them through the winter, especially if she was careful. She had gathered nuts, roots, berries and other edibles from the forest, along with dried meat. Any fresh meat, such as rabbits or other small critters, would be cooked immediately, allowing the dried meat to be saved for when the weather was too bad for them to venture outside.

As a precaution, she had filled several skins of water in case no water flowed when it turned cold enough to freeze it, as was the case where she had lived down below. Each year the river would ice over so thick they could not break through it, even with large rocks. As soon as the weather began to turn cold, they would fill anything that would hold water and place it inside their huts. She did not know if that would be true here in the cave, but decided to take no chances. She had cleaned out gourds to make storage containers out of them and had them sitting neatly to one side of the cave.

"With great patience, she had designed and built a brush cover to hide the opening of the cave, yet allow her access in and out with ease. From the various animals she had killed, she had tanned the hides, giving them warm clothes to wear and rugs to sit on.

"Charlakavos was proud of herself. She had accomplished far more than she thought she was capable of doing. The people of the clan would be surprised to know that she and her child were still alive and living better than most of them.

"One evening, after they'd eaten and Hummingbird had crawled into her bed, Charlakavos sat, staring into the small fire pit, watching the flames flicker back and forth. It was these times that were hard on her. There was no one to talk to except Hummingbird. Little Otter had not been here since the weather had changed.

"The nights were the worst. There was no one to snuggle close to where she would feel warm and safe. Nor was there anyone to assure her things would be all right.

"Later, when she lay on her bed of skins, in her sleep, she

reached out her hand, only to find her daughter laying there. He Who Fishes had turned out to be a coward, sneaking off to leave her at the mercy of the chief and the other clan members, but even so, before Hummingbird was born, he had been a good provider and lover, and she missed him.

"She wondered if he was still alive? If so, was he living alone somewhere, thinking of her and of what he'd done? Or had warriors of another clan killed him? She hoped he had survived and was sorry for deserting her. She wasn't sure how she would feel if one day he happened to stumble onto the cave, but it wasn't something she needed to worry about right now. If it actually happened, she would deal with it accordingly.

"Pulling the skin up close to her chin to cover herself better, she turned on her side and gazed down at Hummingbird who was fast asleep. She was growing so fast. She would be a young woman soon and what would happen then? She knew Hummingbird loved her, but what of a young woman's needs? She had already seen the wanderlust in her young eyes. She was curious about everything – always asking questions about this or that and forever wanting to know about the people down below and why the two of them had to live up here, all alone?

"During one of Little Otter's visits, together, she and Little Otter tried to explain as best they could about, not only the clan, but other clans, and all their beliefs and fears."

'Then why don't they all get together and be one clan? Wouldn't that make them safer from their enemies?' "Hummingbird asked, using the sign language they had developed.

"This was not a question either of the women could answer, except to say that would be a good idea, but both seriously doubted it would ever happen." 'It would take a strong leader,' "Little Otter declared." 'One that all the clans would look up to and respect.'

"Things became even more complicated one day when Charlakavos and Hummingbird were out gathering berries and roots. The day was warm and they stopped by a river to fill their water skins, and take a bath. By now, Hummingbird was as tall as her mother and beginning to fill out, and as they stood, naked, next to the river, Hummingbird's hands began to move rapidly."

'Why is my skin and hair so much lighter than yours? And why are my eyes a different color than yours? Am I not truly your daughter?'

"Charlakavos took Hummingbird by the hand and as they waded out into the river, she told her the entire story without holding anything back, and when she finished, Hummingbird had a blank look on her face. After a moment, Hummingbird dove deep into the river and swam all the way across to the other side and climbed out and sat on the bank, staring at the water.

"Charlakavos sighed. She had dreaded this day, but now that it had come, she could only hope her daughter would understand. Hummingbird was wise for her young age, but still, she had seen only twelve winters and had lived up here on the mountain, away from other people except for Little Otter and the few other women who Little Otter had brought with her on her rare visits. She only brought women who thought as she did and did not approve of the way things had been done by the clan.

"The sun had moved to the far side of the forest when Hummingbird dove into the water and swam back across the river. She hurriedly got dressed, then, without looking at her mother, raced off into the forest, heading in the direction of the cave.

"Charlakavos picked up their baskets and followed, hoping her daughter would be alright. In the past, she had talked about the Yellow Hairs being their enemy, and now Hummingbird found out that one of them was her father. It was a lot for a young girl to understand."

Singing Bird glanced up at the sky and saw the moon was bright and full, surrounded by more stars than she could count. She had been so engrossed in her storytelling that she didn't realize how late it had become.

Most of the dogs had already gone to sleep where they lay, and she saw children using them as pillows, barely able to keep their eyes open. Even the adults were beginning to nod their heads.

"It is getting late and I need my rest," she said by way of ending the storytelling for the night. She promised to continue in the morning. "I will finish the story when we are all awake and fresh." She hoped Father Death would wait that long.

Sparrow assisted her to stand and then walked with her to her hut and fed her a hot drink that tasted sweet. "This will help you sleep," she said as she pulled a robe over Singing Bird's frail body. "I will come by in the morning and we will go to the hill where you can finish the story."

Singing Bird nodded her head, but could barely remember Sparrow leaving. Sparrow had put something in the drink that allowed her to fall into a deep and restful sleep.

CHAPTER FIVE

-

As Singing Bird and Sparrow made their way up to the top of the rise looking out over the small valley, Singing Bird saw her people were already there. Many of them had come early and cooked their morning meal there so they wouldn't miss Singing Bird's arrival. Several small children ran up and walked beside her. A little boy and a little girl who belonged to Trader and Silver Moon came up on each side of her and took her hands in theirs. She smiled down at them and they smiled back. They were twins. The boy had been born a few minutes ahead of his sister and insisted he was the older of the two and therefore the one to be in charge.

"We will help you up the hill," he said in a tone that indicated he was much older than he was and capable of assisting her.

"Thank you," Singing Bird said. "I am getting along in years and your kind assistance is greatly appreciated by both of you."

They beamed with delight and walked with her all the way to the top of the rise and held her hands as she took her seat on the log. When she was seated, they stepped back, grinning up at her, proud of their accomplishment.

The little girl looked up at her and asked, "Are you going to finish telling the story this morning?"

Singing Bird looked at her and said, "I don't know if I will be able to finish before the sun reaches its highest point, for it is a long story and I don't want to leave anything out; but I will try to finish it today, for I have a journey to take that can't be put off much longer. Now, run along back to your parents so I can begin."

The two children darted down the hill to where their mother waited with breakfast cakes and honey, their favorite.

Two little girls ran up the hill with a bowl filled with several kinds of berries and two kinds of sliced melon and presented it to Singing Bird. She took the bowl then shared it with the two girls, saying it was more than she could eat by herself. Berry juice stained their fingers and dripped from their chins as they gobbled down the delicacies, proud to be allowed to eat with the famous storyteller, Singing Bird. They would tell the story over and over during their lives.

When they had gone back down to sit with their parents, Singing Bird stood up and nodded her appreciation to the children's mother, then stretched. She would begin todays storytelling, standing up. She could see the people better, and make better use of her hands to help emphasize certain points.

Sparrow set a water skin next to the tree stump stool and eased back to where she could see and hear. She knew the story and would soon replace Singing Bird, but today was Singing Bird's day and she didn't want to spoil it for her. She hoped someday she would be able to tell the story with the same flare as Singing Bird.

Seeing Singing Bird stand up and stretch, everyone took it as a sign that she was about to resume her story and they got quiet. Even the birds stopped their chirping and turned to look at her.

Singing Bird watched as the children who were normally rambunctious, took their seats on the grass next to their parents, some next to their dogs, waiting to hear the story for the first time.

When all was quiet, Singing Bird cleared her throat and began. "The following years took their toll on Charlakavos, trying to be mother, father, teacher and provider, although by now, Hummingbird had learned to hunt and brought in as much food as her mother did. Hummingbird had come to terms with the fact that she was different and that her father was not of the clan, and with that knowledge hidden away inside her, she began a quest for life that was far beyond any girl her age. She wanted to know and experience everything from hunting to learning about the forest. She wanted to learn about the herbs and medicines, her mother's clan, the other clans and anything else that came into her thoughts. There seemed to be nothing she didn't want to know about or experience.

"Charlakavos did her best and marveled at Hummingbird's ability to learn. Their sign language continued to grow and soon came naturally to both of them. When they had something to say, they would begin by speaking with hand gestures, adding new ones from time to time. Sometimes when Hummingbird wanted to hear her mother's voice, she would indicate by pointing to her mother's mouth and her ear, which was less tedious on Charlakavos and allowed Hummingbird to remember the spoken word, which came in handy when Little Otter and the others were able to come.

"When Little Otter and the other women who came with her saw the hand speak, as they called it, they became curious and wanted to learn to do it too. Over time, they became adept at it enough to converse with Hummingbird, who questioned them about everything. She was like a giant hole that couldn't be filled.

"From Little Otter and the others, they learned that Hawk had persuaded Sleeps and Thinks to go into the forest to check out the rumors that Charlakavos and her brat had been seen snooping around. Sleeps and Thinks was not happy about the idea. He did not trust Hawk. Besides, why should he care if they were still alive as long as they stayed away? But, after much badgering on Hawk's part and upon his insistence, Sleeps and Thinks reluctantly said he would go with him to check it out.

"The morning had been bleak, filled with black clouds, rain and wind. Sleeps and Thinks took this as a bad omen, but by now, Hawk had the others on his side and Sleeps and Thinks had no choice but to go with Hawk on this fools' quest.

"According to Little Otter, several days later, Hawk came back alone and said Sleeps and Thinks had been killed by Charlakavos. He told them they had found where Charlakavos and her whelp were living, but when they tried to approach them, Charlakavos shot their chief in the neck with a strange weapon that threw long shafts of wood at them. He said the chief had died instantly, and then she threw more wooden shafts at him. After removing his shirt made of cougar skin, he showed the people a wound to his arm that he claimed had come from one of her wooden shafts."

'She is in league with demons!' "he shouted." 'We must hunt her down and destroy her before she and the soul seekers sneak up on us during the dark time and kills us all.'

"Hawk had actually clubbed Sleeps and Thinks to death and thrown him into a ravine for the animals to feast on. He made up the story about Charlakavos to cover his own guilt and to further alienate Charlakavos and her child from the clan.

"Of course, none of what he said was true. Charlakavos would never kill Sleeps and Thinks, or anyone else for that matter unless it was in defense of her and Hummingbird's life. But the question in Charlakavos's mind was how did Hawk know about her bow and arrows?

"Little Otter hung her head and said," 'I may have told some of the other women, who do not believe you or Hummingbird are cursed, about the wonderful devices you said came to you in visions. And possibly Hawk overheard some of them talking about you being able to bring down large animals with your bow and arrows, as you call them.'

"Little Otter told them that upon Sleeps and Thinks death, Hawk had taken over as chief and was demanding they find and kill Charlakavos and her brat, and then burn their remains to destroy the evil demons within them.

"At first, Charlakavos could not believe her ears and was ready to pack up and run, but Hummingbird convinced her to stay and fight."

'You are not alone for I can shoot as well as you and I am strong. Plus, I have a trick or two that will scare them away without having to shoot them,' "she said with hand speak.

"Her mother nodded and smiled for she guessed what those tricks might be. She now had seen thirteen winters and was nearly full-grown. Like her yellow haired father, she was tall and slender, and well-muscled from running in the forest each day with her animal friends.

"Little Otter told them of the new name the clan had given Hummingbird. From time to time, the people of the clan had glimpsed her racing through the forest, making no more sound than the cougar or rabbit." 'Silent Runner, is the new name you have been given, for we can see you racing past, but we never hear you.'

"Both Hummingbird and her mother thought this was a good name because in truth, she did love to run and did so almost everywhere she went. And many times, without her mother for Charlakavos could not keep up.

"Hummingbird enjoyed those times when she could be free to run alone in the forest and be with the animals. For some reason, they were not afraid of her, nor was she afraid of them. In fact, she told her mother she could communicate with them just by thinking. She didn't understand how she did it, but only knew she could, and they could communicate with her. The first time it happened, she was next to a watering place getting a drink when a female deer came out of the forest and stopped, ready to bolt if the human moved in her direction. Hummingbird looked at her and thought in her mind," 'It's all right. I will not hurt you. I want to be your friend.'

"As though she could understand Hummingbird, she walked down to the watering place, got a drink, then walked over and put her chin in Hummingbird's hand and leaned closer to get her neck and back rubbed, then looked up at the female human and just as though she had spoken the words, Hummingbird heard the doe say," 'Thank you. You are a good human and we can be friends.' "And from that day on, when Hummingbird was out in the forest alone, deer, wolves, bears, rabbits, and even cougars ran with her.

"The first time Charlakavos saw her daughter come running up to the cave with a cougar running next to her, she was alarmed and looked around for her spear, but before she could grab it, Hummingbird ran up to her and began gesturing with her hands, telling her that the giant mountain cat was their friend, as well as the other animals of the forest.

"Hummingbird took her mother's hand and led her over to the large cat who eyed her cautiously until Hummingbird stared at the mountain lion for a moment, then grinned."

'He said he is glad you are a friend and he will help keep you safe when you go out alone.'

"Charlakavos looked at her daughter and asked," 'You can really talk to him with your mind speak?'

'Yes, mother,' "Hummingbird said with a wide smile." 'I can communicate with all the animals and we are friends.'

'What about the ones we kill to eat?' "Charlakavos asked.

"Hummingbird's hands flew into motion." 'They understand for they too have to kill to survive. It is Mother Nature's law of survival. It is all right as long as we do it only for meat to eat and not just because we like to kill. I explained to all of them that we would never do that. We want to be their friends. Three sleeps ago, I helped his mate deliver her cubs, all nine of them. Oh mother, they are so small and helpless, and beautiful.'

"Charlakavos looked at the mountain lion who was now laying down with his chin on his paws, and then back at her daughter. She was speechless. How could this be? she wondered and then, slowly, it came to her. This was part of the reason the gods had led them here. Why this was happening, she had no idea, but she could not doubt her eyes."

'Come, mother,' "Hummingbird said, taking her mother's hand, leading her over to the big cat laying on the floor of the cave." 'He likes to have his ears scratched. Go ahead,' "she said with a grin.

"Reluctantly at first, Charlakavos reached out and scratched the big cat behind his ears and he relaxed even more, making a purring sound deep inside his chest.

"Charlakavos looked up at her daughter and smiled, then ran her fingers down across his back, giving him a good scratch. Then as though he was a contented child, he rolled over on his back and spread his legs, wanting her to rub his stomach."

'You're not so fearful, after all,' "Charlakavos said, smiling up at Hummingbird.

"For the next ten moons, wild animals came and went in and

out of the cave as though it was their home also. One rainy night, when the lightning was fierce and the wind came howling through the trees, driving the rain down like bullets against their skin, Charlakavos and Hummingbird enjoyed the company of over a hundred animals seeking refuge from the storm. Of course, the cave was a bit crowded, but Hummingbird had made it clear to all the animals that if they wanted to stay, they would have to get along with each other. There would be no fighting or killing. The cave was neutral ground, and all agreed.

"Charlakavos was overwhelmed and wondered what Hawk and the others would think if they could see this.

"Two moons after the storm, Hummingbird was out picking wild berries so they could put them away for when the cold time came. They would be celebrating her fourteenth winter and her womanhood. Not being able to help herself, Hummingbird was sampling almost as many berries as she was putting in her basket. She'd just put a handful of berries in the basket when a wolf came rushing up so quickly that Hummingbird jumped up and drew her knife, but the wolf shook his head and told her through their mind talk, he was not attacking her, but had come to let her know her mother had had an accident.

"Hummingbird sheathed her knife and followed after the wolf as he turned and ran back in the direction he'd come from."

Singing Bird turned and picked up the water skin and took a long drink and as she was sitting the water skin back down, a little girl ran up and handed Singing Bird something on a large leaf. She looked down and saw it was a piece of honey-bread, her favorite.

She smiled and said, "Thank you." The little girl smiled a tight-lipped smile and then motioned for her to eat. When she'd finished, the little girl handed her a piece of moist skin to wipe her fingers and lips with.

When she was finished, she handed the skin back to the little girl, who smiled, showing a wide gap where her four front teeth used to be. She put her hand over her mouth as though she was embarrassed about her missing teeth.

Singing Bird smiled and said, "I remember trading my small teeth for my big ones. You will someday have a beautiful smile."

The little girl giggled and raced down the hill to where her mother, father, sisters and brothers sat.

Singing Bird looked out over the people and said, "One must stop, even during a story as important as this one, for a piece of honey-bread when it is offered."

There was laughter and a nodding of heads.

Renewed strength flowed through Singing Bird's tired body and she took a deep breath. She could see the young ones sitting up, paying more attention, wanting to know what had happened to Charlakavos, and she didn't disappoint them.

CHAPTER SIX

-

"Hummingbird ran up to the edge of the ravine and looked down. There, laying in a heap, was her mother. Throwing caution to the wind, she leaped over the edge and landed half way down, then, slid the rest of the way to the bottom. Turning, she knelt down next to her mother and felt the tears welling up inside her. She reached over and shook her mother, but she did not move. Hummingbird looked down at the still face of her mother and felt that her heart would break. Her mother couldn't be gone to the great beyond, she thought. It was much too soon. She was not ready for her mother to leave her, there was still so much to learn and so many good times to share. Tears flowed freely down her cheeks and dripped from her chin.

"A giant elk walked up next to Hummingbird and with their mind talk, said," 'Put her on my back and I will carry her back to the cave.'

"With great effort and care, Hummingbird lifted her mother into her arms and laid her stomach down across the great elk's back, then followed him as he climbed out of the ravine.

"By the time they got back to the cave, more than a hundred

animals had come out from the forest and were gathered there to pay their respect to Charlakavos. Even though she couldn't mind talk to them like her daughter could, she had become friends with a great many of them and had put medicine on wounds, and during the cold months, had fed many of them.

"The great elk made his way slowly and reverently into the cave and stopped.

"Hummingbird laid out a piece of bear skin to put her mother on, then walked over and stood next to the great elk."

'Thank you,' "she said with her mind speak, tears in her eyes.

"After taking a deep breath to help relieve the pain she felt, she reached up and lifted her mother from the elk's back. She turned and was about to lay her on the bear skin, when her mother gave a great gasp and opened her eyes."

'What happened?' "she asked, looking directly into Hummingbird's eyes.

"A huge sob welled up in Hummingbird's throat and she gulped to catch her breath. Smiling and hugging her mother to her, she thanked the gods, then with gentle hands, she laid her mother on the bear skin bed and with her hand talk, explained what had happened."

'We all thought you had gone to the great beyond,' "she said, and Charlakavos turned her head and looked at the entrance to the cave and saw all the animals jumping up and down, frolicking around like newborns now that she was alive, again. Tears came to her eyes and ran down her cheeks."

'They all came for me?' "she asked, and Hummingbird nodded her head, wiping the tears of joy from her own eyes."

'Help me up. I must thank them,' "she said, but as she tried to turn over to get up, she let out a scream of pain.

"Hummingbird jumped back and looked at her mother." 'What is wrong?'

'I think I must have broken something,' "Charlakavos said, after regaining her composure.

"Hummingbird knelt down next to her mother and examined her left leg and hip. Her hip was black and blue, and swollen. Her leg between the knee and foot was swollen and looked to be broken because it was at a strange angle. Together, they determined she had broken her left leg and maybe her hip in the fall."

'I do not know how to fix your wounds. What am I to do?' "Hummingbird asked in a flash of hand movements, her face a mask of fear and worry."

'It will be all right,' "Charlakavos said." 'I remember what Owl, our medicine man, did when one of our warriors broke his arm during a battle with another clan. We can reset my leg the same way, but first, I want you to go into the forest and look for a tall, green leafed plant with yellow buds. It is called, bitter lettuce. The stem produces a white, milky substance that will help take the pain away,' "she said, without mentioning her hip. She had no idea how to fix a broken hip, but would deal with that when the time came. First, her leg, then she would worry about her hip."

'Where will I find this, bitter lettuce?' "Hummingbird asked."

'I do not know if it grows up this high on the mountain, but if you cannot find it, go down, and if you can, seek out Little Otter without anyone seeing you, and tell her what has happened and what you are looking for, she will know what to do,' "Charlakavos said, patting her daughter's arm.

"Hummingbird was reluctant to leave her mother, but her mother told her she would be alright until she could get back with the pain killer, but to hurry.

"Outside the cave, Hummingbird gave instructions to the animals to stand watch and if her mother cried out in pain, to come find her."

Singing Bird looked around at the little ones and saw they were happy that Charlakavos had not gone to the great beyond, but were sad that she had broken her leg and maybe her hip.

"Did Hummingbird run and get some of that medicine? Was it growing nearby?" a little boy down in front asked.

Singing Bird looked down at him and said, "First, she searched a wide area near the cave, looking for the tall green, leafy plant with the yellow buds, but she couldn't find anything that looked like what her mother had described, so, she hurried back to the cave to check on her mother who was laying quietly on the bear skin bedding."

'Go down the mountain and find Little Otter,' "her mother said," 'and hurry the pain is getting worse.'

"Hummingbird now became the new name she was called by the ones down below, Silent Runner. She had never run so fast in all her life – dodging branches and weaving in and out among the trees. Not even the mountain lion or the bear would have been able to keep up with her. For the first time in her young life, she was very afraid.

"She had never actually been down as far as where the clan made their huts, but in the distance ahead of her, she could make them out and slowed down to a walk when she got close. Her eyes constantly searched all around her to make sure someone out gathering berries or a male out hunting game hadn't spotted her. She edged closer, stopping behind trees to scout the land ahead of her. She was looking between the branches of a large bush when she saw Little Otter come out of one of the huts carrying a water container.

"Circling around, Silent Runner was waiting when Little Otter approached the river. After checking to make sure they were alone, Silent Runner stepped out from behind a tree and beckoned Little Otter to come closer.

"Little Otter was surprised to see her and rushed over, looking around, nervously.

"When they were very close, Silent Runner used her sign language and told Little Otter what had happened and asked if she knew where she could find some of the plants her mother had asked for.

"Little Otter's face was grave and she said," 'I know of some near my hut, but we must be cautious. Go back to your mother and comfort her. Make her some broth and tell her I will bring the medicine as soon as I can get away,' "she said with worry in her voice.

"Silent Runner gave Little Otter a hug, then turned and raced back up the mountain as though it was flat ground.

"Little Otter hurriedly filled the water jug and took it back to her hut. Hawk was ranting and raving about something and had most of the clan under his spell, which allowed Little Otter to sneak out the backside of her hut and seek out the plant she would need; also taking some skin for binding the leg if they could get it back in place.

"Not far from her hut, she found a small cluster of the plants growing and picked all of them and put them in the sack with the bindings; then hurried up the mountain before anyone noticed she was missing.

"Silent Runner made her mother broth from herbs and dried meat, and she was sipping on it when Little Otter came out of the forest and stopped, her eyes growing wide. She was staring eye to eye with the biggest mountain lion and bear she had ever seen. The mountain lion was making a growling noise that made Little Otter want to turn and run, but instead, she called out in a loud whisper," 'Silent Runner...'

"Silent Runner ran to the entrance of the cave and looked out. When she saw all the animals staring at Little Otter, she smiled and said in her mind talk," 'It's alright, she is a friend and one who has come to help Charlakavos.'

"Little Otter watched in awe as the mountain lion stopped growling and stepped back. The bear sat back on his haunches and began to scratch himself, no longer paying any attention to her, while the other animals turned away and went back to what they were doing before she arrived."

'How did you do that?' "Little Otter asked when she got inside the cave.

"Silent Runner laughed her soundless laugh and let her hands speak for her and said," 'Somehow I can communicate with the animals through our... through our minds.'

'And they don't hurt you?' "Little Otter asked, overwhelmed by the thought."

'Oh no. They are friends with both, mother and me,' "Silent Runner said, proudly and matter-of-factly.

"Little Otter had a hard time understanding how you could be friends with a bear or a mountain lion – a little rabbit, maybe, but large animals that would eat you? She was amazed that Silent Runner could do the things she did and so effortlessly.

"Charlakavos gave a slight groan, which broke Little Otter out of her state of amazement and she rushed over and examined her friend."

'Yes, her leg is broken, but I think her hip is only dislocated.'

"Little Otter looked down at Charlakavos and said," 'I will make up the medicine to help with the pain then we will put your leg back together.'

"Charlakavos nodded and lay back so her friend could do what needed to be done.

"After squeezing all the substance from the plants, she mixed it with some of the broth and handed it to Charlakavos and said," 'drink this all down, then lay back and try to relax as the medicine relieves your pain. When you feel no more pain, I will put your leg back together. There may be some slight pain when we do, but it should go away quickly.'

'Thank you, my friend,' "Charlakavos said.

"Without another word, she drank the potion down and gave a small shudder, then handed the bowl to Silent Runner before laying back on the bear skin rug and closing her eyes.

Singing Bird stopped and once again, lifted the water skin to her lips and drank thirstily.

The sun was nearing full overhead and knew she would have to stop soon so they could prepare their noonday meal. Even storytelling had to stop during mealtime. Her growling stomach let her know she was in need of nourishment. The only thing she'd eaten today was the bowl of berries and melon given to her by her friend, Bright Star, who, along with others, would make enough to share with her.

She looked at the sky again and judged she still had a little more time before their mid-day meal and smiled down at the children in the front who were waiting anxiously for her to continue.

'Mother,' "Silent Runner said, but there was no response. The medicine had put her into a deep sleep."

'It is time,' "Little Otter said, then instructed Silent Runner to hold her mother's shoulders so she would stay stable while her leg was being put back together.

"Silent Runner did as she was asked and watched as Little Otter moved closer and knelt down, just beyond her mother's foot.

Then, when Silent Runner had taken her mother by the shoulders, Little Otter reached out and took Charlakavos by the foot with both hands and yanked.

"Charlakavos gave a slight groan, but otherwise, did not move. Little Otter looked at Silent Runner, who was staring wide eyed at her mother's leg. It now looked straight again.

"Quickly, Little Otter run her hand lightly over the leg, then up to the hip. After a moment she looked up and smiled." 'Everything is back as it belongs. Now we must bind the leg to hold it in place until it heals,' "she said, reaching for some small pieces of wood and the binding she had brought with her.

"Silent Runner watched, missing nothing as Little Otter bound up the leg using the pieces of wood to hold the leg straight, then binding the wood against the leg with the leather straps so the broken part could not move and be injured again."

'She will need to keep this on for two moons before walking on it again,' "Little Otter said as she stood up and looked around."

'She will also need a walking stick to keep any weight off her broken leg during the healing time – one that will fit under her arm and shoulder.'

"Silent Runner understood and went outside and was gone only a short time when she returned with a piece of wood resembling a crutch. All it needed was to be shortened to fit her mother's height. And for added comfort, she bound a piece of rabbit skin to the part that fit under her mother's armpit."

'Excellent!' "Little Otter cried when she saw the finished

product.

"Pleased with herself, Silent Runner turned toward her mother and saw her smiling at her.

"She looked down at her leg and asked," 'Will I be able to walk, again?'

"Little Otter knelt down next to her friend and handed her more of the potion and said," 'In two moons. But in the meantime, you must try to move around as little as you can – but if you have to go somewhere, Silent Runner has fixed something for you to use.'

"Charlakavos looked up at her daughter and smiled. She was proud of how she had acted responsibly."

'Now, I must get back before I am missed,' "Little Otter said." 'Hawk is suspicious of me, already. He knows you and Silent Runner have made a home up here, somewhere, and remembers that we were friends. Several times he has put the question to me, but I tell him I know nothing. He continues to search for you, but his luck has not been good. He has offered a reward to anyone who knows where you are and tells him, so I must be wary with my comings and goings. I have to watch so that I am not followed, for most of the others are afraid of Hawk and will do anything to gain his favor.'

"At the edge of the clearing, just before she entered the forest, Little Otter watched as the animals disappeared back into the forest."

'If you see a bear following you, do not be alarmed. I have told him to see you safely back,' "Silent Runner said with her hand talk," 'and I cannot thank you enough. If you ever need my help, you have only to ask.'

"Little Otter looked at Silent Runner and marveled. Overnight, she had become a young woman." 'I will come back when I can.' "And with that, she turned and walked into the forest.

"Off to the side and out of sight, a large bear kept pace with her, sniffing the air from time to time to make sure no other humans were nearby.

"During the next two moons, Silent Runner learned a lot about what it meant to be an adult. Even though she protested, Silent Runner did for her mother as though she was a child. She cooked, she cleaned, she gathered herbs and plants, hunted game for their pot, and tanned the hides. She did everything her mother used to do and Charlakavos had to admit, she did it as good as she could do it. Silent Runner even removed the binding from her mother's leg from time to time, so she could carefully clean it and then rebind it.

"Little Otter had been to see them twice and each time, praised Silent Runner for how well she was doing. On her third visit, she was chuckling and told them that, shortly after leaving the clan, from a short distance behind her, she heard a large bear growl loudly, and then heard a woman scream." 'Whoever it was, made much noise running back to the clan,' "she said, trying hard not to laugh." 'I will need a good story to tell when I get back; something Hawk cannot find fault with.'

"Silent Runner thought for a minute, then said with her hands," 'You were out looking for the medicine plants and saw a bear and ran and climbed a tree and was afraid to come down after hearing it growl and a woman scream. Only later did you find it safe to come down.'

"Little Otter looked at Silent Runner and thought, how smart she was, and at such a young age, too. Yes, it would be a good story if she needed one."

CHAPTER SEVEN

-

"It had been a long, cold winter with much snow and Silent Runner was tired of being cooped up inside the cave. She wanted to run through the forest and feel the air blowing her hair out behind her, feel her muscles straining from stretching them. She wanted to be free of the cave. She missed her animal friends. She loved her mother, but all these moons, stuck here in the cave was beginning to make her feel like a prisoner.

"Her mother was able to do for herself now and could get around without the crutch, but did so with a limp. Even though it wasn't painful, her hip and leg were never the same. Charlakavos never complained - she was glad to be alive and watch her daughter grow into adulthood. The winter, for her, had been good. She had been able to teach her daughter many things about being an adult.

"Silent Runner had become a woman during the cold time and her mother had held the womanhood celebration without the help of a medicine man, or anyone else. She would have liked to have had Little Otter and some of the others here to help celebrate this joyous occasion, but there had been a heavy snow and it had become so cold you could not be outside for more than a few minutes. It was as the gods wanted it, she supposed.

"Charlakavos could not be prouder of her daughter. She was tall; taller than her, and her light skin had turned to a bronze color, making her steel blue eyes and blonde hair all the more prominent. She was perfect in every way.

"She had not seen her husband or her sons since leaving the clan, but had learned from Little Otter on her last visit that He Who Fishes had been found, floating in the river. And her sons, Little Otter said with sadness in her voice, stood with Hawk and were feared by the other clan members. Hawk and his pack of would-be warriors reigned over the clan with brute force." 'You should be glad you are not there. It is no longer a good place to live.'

'How can they call themselves warriors if they have never fought against a real enemy?' "Silent Runner asked."

'Oh, they strut around and brag about what they will do to the Yellow Hairs if they ever come back and the others believe them,' "Little Otter had said."

'Do they ever ask about me or their sister?' "Charlakavos asked meekly.

"Little Otter had lowered her head and said," 'I am sorry to say, no. They believe as Hawk tells them to believe. It is a shame for they are tall and strong and handsome.'

"That visit had been just before the weather turned cold again and the snow so deep you could not walk.

"Fortunately, it did not last long, but as they learned, bad weather could come at any time up here.

"The snow and cold weather had not been gone a full moon when they saw the black smoke rising in the air. It looked to be coming from near where the clan's huts should be."

'I will go and see what has happened,' "Silent Runner said with her hand talk."

'Be careful and do not let them see you,' "Charlakavos said.

"When Silent Runner got close, the pungent smell of burning huts and human flesh assaulted her nostrils. Even Cougar and Bear, who now went everywhere with her, could not tolerate the smell and warned her not to go any closer, but Silent Runner had to know what had happened.

"With great caution, she approached the area and saw nothing but what was left of the burned huts, smoldering in the afternoon sun. Here and there, she saw the dead bodies of male warriors, but no women. She had to swallow hard to keep down the bile that welled up in her throat. She had never seen dead humans before, and never ones who died in battle, with spears still sticking out of their bodies, or their heads cut off. She was about to leave when she heard a groan and turned, looking to see where it had come from, but there was only silence. She was searching the ruins for where the sound had come from when she heard the groan again. It seemed to be coming from beneath a large piece of burning wood.

"With the use of a large stick, she hefted the wood from the body beneath it and to her surprise, there was Little Otter, curled up in a ball, her hair nearly all burned off, and she was covered from head to toe with large splotches where her body had been burned.

"Out of two long poles and pieces of binding she found, Silent Runner made a litter of sorts and tied it to Bear, then lifted the whimpering body of Little Otter and laid her on it."

'You will be all right,' "Silent Runner said with her hand talk, but didn't think, in her condition, she understood since her eyes were closed because of the burn marks on her face.

"With no effort on Bear's part, he pulled Little Otter up the mountain.

"Later, in the cave, her mother administered herbal medicine to the burns and gave her some of the pain medicine from the long green plants with the yellow buds. The strong medicine pulled Little Otter's eyes closed and for the first time since being burned, she rested without pain. The following morning, Little Otter opened her eyes and smiled. She took some broth, then went back to sleep.

"Later, after the sun had gone down, with gasping breath, Little Otter told them," 'The Yellow Hairs came... they raided us just before... sunrise. We were asleep and not prepared. They killed anyone who tried to resist... I pulled a piece of skin over me and curled up next to the wall of my hut... apparently, they thought I was nothing more than a pile of skins. When they... burned my hut down... the wall fell on me and I couldn't get out. I was sure I was going to die along with the others. I was in so much pain, that...'

"Charlakavos told her not to talk any longer and that she should get more rest. There would be plenty of time for talk when she felt better.

"Later, outside the cave, Charlakavos and Silent Runner

talked at length about what had happened and what would happen to the ones who were taken away as prisoners."

'They will make slaves of the men and sell them to people in lands far from here, across the great water. As for the women... it will not be a good life. They will be used by any of the men who have a need and they will be treated like slaves; even beaten if they do not do as they are told. The younger ones will be sold or traded to whoever can afford to pay the price for them.'

'When you were a captive, did my father beat you and treat you badly?' "Silent Runner asked.

"Charlakavos looked at the sky, remembering her time with the Yellow Hairs and gave a sigh."

'No, I was one of the lucky ones. Although I was just a captive, no better than any of the other slaves, for some reason, your father kept me for himself and didn't allow me to be passed around. I think he knew I would run away; but even so, he did not put me under guard, or tie me up at night like many of the others were. I think he hoped I would stay because he treated me better. I did not know I was with child or maybe I...'

"Confusion filled Silent Runner's face as she interrupted her mother." 'Mother, it is all very confusing. Why would he keep you for his own and then allow you to escape?'

'I do not know,' "Charlakavos said after a moment of thought." 'I can only believe the gods had something to do with it so you could be born.'

"Silent Runner looked at her mother and sighed." 'I do not

understand. I am not special. I am no one. I am just a female who was cursed by the gods and cannot make sounds. I was banned by the people for that and for being of two different worlds. What could the gods want of me?'

"Charlakavos sighed." 'Over the many seasons, I have asked that very same question. I do not know why we are here, except I do believe the gods have a reason. What that reason is, I do not know. But, I do believe you are very special and when the time comes, they will reveal to us what their plan is and why we were sent here to live, far away from the clan.'

"Silent Runner looked at her mother and said," 'If we had been living with the clan when the Yellow Hairs came, would we not have been killed or taken captive?'

"Charlakavos looked over her shoulder at her friend, Little Otter and said," 'Yes. Why we have been spared I do not know, but I am glad you will not have to experience what I did.'

"Little Otter groaned in her sleep. Silent Runner and her mother went back inside the cave to check on her. Silent Runner stared down at the person she called her aunt and felt anger well up in her for what the Yellow Hairs had done to her. Even though she was of mixed blood, she was clan, like her mother.

CHAPTER EIGHT

-

"The following morning, the sun was shining brightly when Charlakavos opened her eyes and looked around. She had stayed up late, tending her friend - putting ointment on her burns and giving her more pain medicine so she could rest.

"Glancing toward the entrance of the cave, she saw Silent Runner looking out over the forest. She had her bow and arrows slung over her shoulder and carried a spear in her left hand. Her knife was hanging from her waist on her right side and an axe on her left side. She turned when her mother approached.

"Charlakavos looked at her daughter and asked," 'Why are you dressed this way? Are you going hunting?'

"Silent Runner looked her mother in the eyes and said," 'In a way. Last night I had a vision telling me why I have been spared and what I am to do.'

"Charlakavos felt a chill run down her spine."

'I am to go after the people of the clan and bring them back,' "Silent Runner said matter of factly."

'But... but, how can you do that? You are only one against many and they are trained warriors – large men who would not care that you are a female and would kill you or worse, take you captive. And why should you care about the people of the clan? They turned us out because you are half Yellow Hair. Why should you want to do this?'

"Silent Runner shook her head and with her hands she said," 'I do not know, mother. The vision only said I must make war on the Yellow Hairs and free the ones who have been taken.'

'And how will you do that? And even if you succeed, what will you do then?' "Charlakavos, asked, feeling the panic rising inside her."

"Charlakavos knew in her heart she was fighting a losing battle. Her daughter had been chosen by the gods to do this thing. She could only hope they would stay with her and protect her."

'I do not know that, either,' "Silent Runner said, looking into her mother's eyes."

'Maybe you should wait until tomorrow, in case the gods change their minds,' "Charlakavos pleaded.

"Silent Runner smiled at her mother and embraced her, holding her tight, hoping this would not be the last time." 'I must go, mother. The gods have spoken.'

'I know you must do what the gods ask, but...' "Charlakavos said, trying to find a reason to keep her daughter here where it was safe."

'Do not worry, mother,' "Silent Runner said, with more conviction than she felt." 'I will do what I must, then return here, to you and Little Otter. Stay with her and make her well again. If the gods are willing, I will see you soon.'

"And with that, Silent Runner turned and marched off down the mountain, disappearing into the forest.

"Charlakavos smiled, and felt a little better when she saw Bear and Cougar fall in behind her daughter.

"For a long while, Charlakavos stood at the entrance of the cave, staring into the forest below, hoping to see her daughter coming back. She didn't understand how the gods could let a girl of only fourteen winters challenge the Yellow Hairs. They were full grown men - fierce warriors who gave no quarter.

"Her mind went back to the time when she had been their captive and first saw the big boat they had sailed across the great waters. She learned they had counted thirty-four suns before seeing land and during that time they had endured three storms. The Yellow Hairs had fought Mother Nature and were victorious. If they could do that, how could a young girl hope to go to war with them?

"Charlakavos heard a groan and turned back into the cave and her friend, Little Otter. Worrying would solve nothing. Her daughter's life was in the hands of the gods now and there was nothing she could do but pray they would watch over her.

CHAPTER NINE

-

"Silent Runner had no idea what she was to do and decided the first and most logical thing to do would be to go back down to the burned ruins and try to find a trail to follow. Surely, a group as large as they must be would leave plenty of prints to follow. At least she hoped so.

"As she ran, her thoughts turned to what her mother had asked her about why she should care about a people who turned them out just because she was different. And how was she, a lone girl, going to fight against an enemy she knew nothing about, except that they were large male warriors, who to the best of her knowledge had never lost a battle.

"But even as she thought the words, she knew she would have to find a way to defeat them – the gods had willed it.

"Halfway down the mountain, Wolf, Bear and Cougar caught up to Silent Runner for she was just jogging and they could keep up with her at that pace."

'Do not fear, little one,' "Cougar said in his mind speak," 'we will help protect you.'

"Silent Runner smiled and no longer felt alone and her

courage grew. Even though she was no longer alone, and could summon a large group of animals to help her, a frontal attack would not be the way to do it; too many animals would be killed. No, she would need the cunning of the mountain lion, the strength of the bear and the speed and determination of the wolf."

Singing Bird stopped and reached for the water skin, and as she drank, she could see the children staring up at her. She knew she must tell the story as it happened, but she must also choose her words wisely so as not to scare the young ones hearing the story for the first time.

After quenching her thirst, Singing Bird replaced the water skin, then sat down on the tree stump and raised her hands. Smiling, she began again.

"Silent Runner took her time, circling the area. On the south edge of where the camp used to be, she found where all the captives had been gathered. She could easily tell the difference in the footprints. The members of the clan wore moccasins, while the Yellow Hairs wore a different kind of footwear like nothing she'd ever seen, but no matter, they made larger tracks that were deeper and were easier to follow.

"She noticed that the captives had been taken toward the rising sun by only part of the Yellow Hairs, while another group of them had moved off to the north and for a moment, she was undecided what to do."

'If it was me,' "Cougar said with his mind speak," 'I would follow the ones from the clan. They are the ones you came to rescue.'

'But I would keep a wary eye out,' "Bear added.

"The large, gray wolf sniffed the air and said," 'I agree. Follow the ones you came to rescue, but keep a lookout for the others who have gone to the north. They could return at any time.'

'Do you suppose they went in search for another clan to take captive?' "Silent Runner asked."

'Yes, that would be my guess,' "Cougar interjected.

"So off they went, following the tracks of the ones headed toward the rising sun. For five suns, they followed their tracks through the forest, stopping at the sites where they had made camp the night before, finding the land filled with their leavings and was disgusted by their lack of caring for the land.

"Even Silent Runner could not stand the smells they left behind. At two of their camps, she found dead bodies, both, older women. Silent Runner said a silent prayer for them, after placing their bodies on a pile of brush and setting it on fire, sending them to the great beyond with dignity.

"Still inexperienced in warfare, Silent Runner didn't realize the smoke from the burial fires might be seen by the ones she was following, so she was almost taken by surprise when four of the Yellow Hairs were sent back along the trail to see where the smoke was coming from and who caused it.

"Fortunately for Silent Runner, the wild animals had even better hearing and smell than she did and warned her of the danger."

'How can I fight four warriors if they are all together?' "she asked her companions.

"Bear ambled up and said," 'Stay on the trail and do not worry. I have a plan.'

"Silent Runner began to walk toward the sun at a steady, but slower pace than her normal jogging run. Her companions disappeared into the forest and she felt alone and vulnerable, but she trusted the wisdom of Bear and continued on down the trail.

'Vell, vat have vee here?' "one of the yellow haired warriors said when they came face to face with Silent Runner."

'How could vee have missed this von?' "another one of them said as they circled her and looked at her with lust in their eyes.

"Silent Runner stood very still, but her eyes watched their every move and was ready to fight if they came too close."

'This von is different,' "one of them said." 'See her eyes, her hair and her skin. I tink she is da product of our last raid.'

"At this, they all laughed."

'Ya, looks like Sven's verk,' "the tall one with a scar down across his cheek, said."

'Ya, she even looks and dresses like him,' "another of them said."

'Vat are ya called by?' "the short dumpy one asked and when she only stared at him, he drew back his hand to strike her to make her talk; but his eyes grew wide for he was staring at a knife that suddenly appeared in her hand."

'Vell, dis von is fiesty. I like dat,' "he said.

"The others laughed and the tall one with the scar said," 'Vee vill have fun vit dis von, but ven vee have finished, vee vill leave her carcass for the vild animals ta feast on. I don't tink Sven vould like it if vee brought his bastard child back all used up.'

"Although Silent Runner could not understand their tongue, their intentions were clear, and she felt her muscles tense up. She took a deep breath, preparing herself for the fight, wondering where her friends were.

"She didn't have to wonder long, for only a few heartbeats later, Bear roared onto the path and drove his shoulder into the side of the one with the scar and knocked him down – and before the others could react, Wolf attacked the short, stocky one, while Cougar leaped onto the back of the one closest to him – leaving only one of them to face Silent Runner.

"In all the excitement, the one left, a tall, slender Yellow Hair not much older than Silent Runner, was busy looking at the wild animal attack and didn't see the girl had notched an arrow onto the string of her bow and had it pointed at him.

"Not sure what to do, he turned to flee into the forest but hadn't gone more than a few steps when a large elk drove his antlers into the young man's stomach and lifted him into the air, then shook its head, sending the dead warrior into a patch of briars.

"When it was over, Silent Runner walked into the forest and leaned against a tree and was sick. This was the first time she had seen what war was really like and she didn't like it one bit."

'We are no better that they are,' "she told her companions with her mind speak when they joined her on the trail, while shaking her head back and forth.

"Bear had a puzzled look on his face and ambled over and sat back on his haunches and asked," 'What other way is there? We are fighting for not only our lives but also the lives of the others. These warriors would have done you much harm, then killed you and left your remains out here without a decent send off to the great beyond.'

'We know you are young and have not experienced this kind of life. That is why we are here to help you and protect you if we can; but there will be times when you must fight to stay alive so you can help the others,' "Cougar explained.

"Silent Runner nodded her head, realizing what he'd said to her was true. Even though she had only been gone for a short time, she missed her mother and life at the cave, where things like this never happened. Why had the gods chosen her to do their work? she wondered. From now on she must think like a male warrior, not a female who hated war.

"That night and from then on, she would no longer camp where the enemy had camped for fear they would send more warriors. Instead, she found places with her friends and bedded down with them, choosing to eat only herbs and berries. Cougar, Bear or Wolf never mentioned it, but they saw how she handled being among them and appreciated it. Both, Wolf and Cougar would go away from the camp to hunt and satisfy their hunger cravings, while Bear shared his meals with Silent Runner, filling himself on berries."

CHAPTER TEN

-

Singing Bird knew this next part of the story could not actually be sworn to, but it added so much to the telling that it couldn't be left out. And no one had ever questioned the fact that it was something she had conjured up in her mind as to what the Yellow Hairs were doing and thinking. The people assumed it had been part of the story told by Silent Runner, and a portion of it had been, but Singing Bird had had to fill in the parts Silent Runner hadn't said anything about.

"The leader of the Yellow Hairs, Sven, stared up the mountainside, wondering what had happened to the men he'd sent to check on the dark smoke rising out of the forest near where he thought one of their old camps had been. They had been gone two days and he was worried.

"Sven was a tall, powerfully built man who intimidated people just by his presence and rarely did anything bother him, but this time a rumbling in his stomach told him things were not as they should be.

"He looked around at the captives, studying them. In all the years they had been raiding and taking captives to sell or trade as slaves, not one of them had ever been a worthy opponent. They had no leadership; no weapons to speak of, and when it came to fighting; they had no stomach for it."

'So vat happened ta da four soldiers I sent ta check on da smoke?' "Sven said to himself." 'Did dey run inta problems, or maybe dey ver yust having a good time vit der new captives?'

"He knew the latter could be true, for Albin cared not whether they were male or female, and all of them were in their prime, especially when there were females involved..."

Singing Bird let this last part sink in as she took another sip of water, then continued.

"Sven had seen more than fifty winters and was feeling the effects of the many raids he'd led over the years and vowed this would be his last. Next season, he would step down and let one of the others take over. He would stay home and watch over all the lonely women left behind.

"After they had been gone four sunsets, the yellow haired warriors began to talk among themselves, wondering what could have happened to them.

"Sven could not tolerate such ramblings so he called one of his seasoned veterans over and spoke to him of his concerns."

'Erick, vat do ya make of Albin and da udders not returning yet?'

"Erick was nearly as large as Sven and was a seasoned warrior who would more than likely take Sven's place next year. He was carrying a gourd filled with a fermented liquid and lifted it to his lips and took a long pull before answering."

'Ya, da men are gettin' restless and babblin' on about da udders bein' gone so long. I heard von of dem say he tot somethin' bad had happened and maybe da gods had abandoned dem, but my insides tells me it vas somethin' else. If dey had vanted ta play loose vit der captives dey vould have done so and vould have been back before now. Ya, dat is vat I tink.'

"Sven reached out and took the gourd from Erick's hand and drank deeply."

'I agree,' "he said." 'My stomach also tells me something is vrong. I vant ya ta pick tree men and go see vat has happened. Arm yerselves and take no chances.

'You may even meet up vit Lars comin' back from his raid. If ya need help, he vill have plenty of men.'

"Erick placed his hand on his leader's shoulder and said," 'Rest vell, my commander, and consider it done. Vee leave at first light.'

CHAPTER ELEVEN

-

"High winds were pushing dark clouds over the mountain area where Silent Runner and her companions were traveling, promising rain when Cougar stopped and lifted his nose in the air, then turned and alerted Silent Runner that more of the enemy was coming up the trail."

'What do you want us to do?' "Bear asked, sitting back on his haunches while he scratched his stomach.

"Silent Runner thought for a moment before a smile crossed her face; then with her mind talk, she told them her plan and watched as they disappeared into the forest.

"When they had gone, Silent Runner looked around and found a tree with a lot of foliage where she could hide. Then, nimble as a squirrel, she climbed the tree and found a spot high among the branches where she could see, but not be seen, yet giving her a good field of fire, she began to pick pinecones and put them into the pouch hanging at her side.

"She had to wait only a few minutes before she heard them. They sounded like a flock of geese. Silent Runner figured they were so used to just storming into a clan and doing as they liked without opposition that they didn't feel the need to make a silent approach.

"A hole in the dark clouds allowed the moon to send its light into the clearing below her and she watched as they stopped to pass a gourd among themselves, laughing and staggering around from the effects of the fermented liquid.

"Silent Runner knew nothing of fermented drink and wondered how men who staggered around and fell down a lot as they were doing, could be conquering warriors? They didn't look like much to her, she thought as she smiled and put her plan into action.

"She notched an arrow onto her bowstring and pulled it back, took careful aim, then let the arrow fly.

"Erick stopped dead in his tracks as an arrow drove itself into the ground between his feet. Looking around to try and see his opponent, he drew his long sword, holding it at the ready.

'Vat ya doin'?' "One of the men asked as he walked up and looked at Erick like he'd lost his mind." 'I don't see nobody ta fight.'

'Look between my feet and tell me vat ya see.' "Erick said in a whisper.

"The young warrior looked down and instantly sobered. Drawing an axe from where it hung at his side, he too, let his eyes scan the forest.

"When the others saw Erick and Adrian draw their weapons, they, too, sobered up as best they could, and armed themselves, ready for battle, but none of them could see anyone to fight. Then out of the night, all around them, the air came alive with the hair-raising sound of hundreds of wolves howling.

"As they bunched up and put their backs to each other, forming a circle, their weapons at the ready, the mournful cry of mountain lions also filled the air."

'Vat is going on?' "Lucas, a brute of a man with a long red beard and bushy hair asked.

"Next, what sounded like a forest filled with large bears growling assaulted their ears, causing them to draw into a tighter circle."

'Der are evil forces here,' "Adrian told them as chills ran down his back." 'I say vee should go back. Vee cannot fight spirits.'

"Erick didn't believe in spirits and wasn't ready to turn back just yet, but even so, he knew something wasn't right. Bears, wolves and mountain lions were sworn enemies and didn't hang around together. Yet, he had heard all three, if that's really what they had been. The possibility of evil spirits was growing in his mind."

'Hold yer positions,' "Erick said with as strong a voice as he could muster." 'I am not yet convinced dey are spirits.'

"Just as a dark cloud passed in front of the moon, they felt pinecones raining down on them. Lucas was struck in the eye, one stuck itself to Erick's cheek and Adrian felt one strike him on the ear. They immediately raised their shields to ward off the pinecones."

'Trees do not trow der pinecones. Vat is happening? I agree vit Adrian, der are evil spirits in dis part of da forest.'

"Just then the cloud passed and they drew in deep breaths. Except for the way behind them, mountain lions, bears and wolves, all snarling and growling, surrounded them; many, many more than they knew they could win a fight against.

"Seemingly out of nowhere, arrows struck Erick and Adrian in the arms that held their weapons."

'Da forest is shooting arrows at us! Run, before vee all die!' "Adrian screamed as he ran back down the trail, with the rest keeping pace with him. And suddenly, they were gone.

"After they disappeared, Silent Runner climbed down from her place in the tree and retrieved the arrows that were stuck in the ground, then turned and with her mind talk, thanked all of the animals for their help.

"As she watched them disappear into the forest, Cougar turned to her and said with his mind talk," 'We won't be far away if you need our help, again.'

'I know, and I thank you,' "she said back at him, wondering what she would have to do to rescue the people. Like the clan people, the Yellow Hairs seemed to be afraid of spirits. She wondered if somehow, she could use that against them. She didn't actually believe in evil spirits, but wasn't totally sure, and it did not matter, as long as they did.

"Turning, she followed the tracks down the mountain. She was sure from the stories her mother had told her, they were headed for where the land stopped and the great water began. She had never seen the great water, but her mother had, and had described it as something to see." 'You cannot see the other side, it is so wide,' "her mother had told her." 'And it has a salty taste to it and will make you sick if you drink it.'

"Silent Runner had seen melted snow, water in the river and even water in a lake, and pools here and there, but had a hard time understanding a lake so big you couldn't see across it. And why would it taste like salt? she wondered. She figured she still had much to learn about the world around her. So far, her world had consisted of the area around the mountaintop where she and her mother called, home.

"The forest was starting to get dark and her stomach was beginning to growl as she looked around for a place to spend the night – a place well-hidden so that she could have a small fire."

CHAPTER TWELVE

-

"In the light of the large bonfire, Sven looked at the arrows that had been in Erick and Adrian's arms and shook his head. There were no markings to tell him who had made them. They were just plain arrows with no designs on them like the ones they made.

"Sven didn't believe in spirits either, but the tale his men told was undeniably strange."

'Trees do not shoot arrows. Der had ta be a varrior hidden der,' "he said with a conviction he didn't fully feel."

'Vell, maybe,' "Erick said." 'But vat about all dem animals dat are sworn enemies bandin' tagater, ready ta attack us? I saw'em. Der vas mountain lions, bears and wolves, all standin' side by side, growlin' at us.'

'Ya. Maybe ya saw somethin', but are ya sure dey ver real? I mean... did any of dem attack ya?' "Sven wanted to know.

"Erick thought about it, looking around at the others who just shrugged their shoulders, then turned back to Sven."

'No, dey didn't attack us, but dey looked and sounded real enough – and dem arrows vee got shot vit, ya, dey ver sure enough real, an vee got da wounds ta prove it.'

"Sven couldn't deny their wounds were real, but he still wasn't convinced spirits were involved. In his mind, he knew there had to be some other explanation; he just didn't know what it could be.

"The sky turned black with huge storm clouds and lightning. Thunder rolled across the sky. Sven had wanted to go back with a war party and find this unknown enemy, to prove to his men that it wasn't spirits, but the coming of the storm pushed that thought from his mind. He knew the rain would make it impossible to find the tracks of the ones who did this, and without proof, he would not be able to convince his men that it hadn't been evil spirits that attacked them, but only desperate clansmen who wanted to scare them into leaving. The only real question was the wild animals.

"When the rain began to fall, Sven, along with his men, all hurried to their tents to wait until the storm passed, leaving only a few men to guard the prisoners who had no protection from the onslaught of the wind and rain and stood huddled together.

"Hawk sat, propped against a tree, his jaw clenched and his eyes burning fire as the rain pounded against his head and ran down his face. He had talked so brave before the Yellow Hairs had come, making himself sound like an invincible god, telling the people how he would not allow the Yellow Hairs to invade them again. He had even bragged about his fighting skills. But when they arrived in the middle of the night, like cowards, while he was in his bed, he had had no chance to prepare; no chance to stand against them, but that was not what the people believed. He could see it in their eyes. And this time, the Yellow Hairs did not just raid the encampment and take a few of the young men and all of the young women; they took everyone except for the very old or the ones who resisted. To insult him even more, they had burned everything to the ground and left the dead for the animals of the forest to feast on. And all he did was stand and watch.

"Earlier today, one of the warriors from his own council, the brother to the one called Hummingbird, or Silent Runner, the one he had gotten banished, had spit on him as he passed by. All his plans and dreams were gone. What these Yellow Hairs would do with him he did not know, but inside, he knew it would not be good.

"He cared not what happened to the others, but only for himself. Maybe he could strike a bargain with their leader, Sven. But what did he have to bargain with? Nothing he could think of. His only reasoning was, he was the leader of the clan and should not be treated like a slave.

"Hawk stood up and stepped to the side, under a branch that afforded him a little more protection from the rain. He stared at the tents where the Yellow Hairs sat dry and protected from the storm - laughing and drinking from their gourds.

"Something had happened that made him curious. They had seen smoke coming out of the trees some distance up the mountain, and the leader, Sven, had sent four of his warriors out to investigate. After four sunsets, when they did not return, he sent out four more. They were not gone long when they came running back onto the beach, wild eyed and scared. A weapon like the ones the Yellow Hairs carried had wounded two of them and Hawk wondered how could this be? He knew none of the clan had weapons of that sort, nor any of the other clans he knew of. It was very puzzling. But, what if there was someone out there who could fight against them?"

Singing Bird looked out over the small valley and saw that every face had a slight smile of knowing on their lips. Most of them had heard the story more than once, but never tired of hearing it for it was of how their great nation had taken roots.

Taking advantage of the small break in the story, Singing Bird took another sip from the water skin before continuing. The cool water felt good on her throat and she felt herself relax. After setting the water skin back on the ground, she resumed her storytelling.

"In his wildest thoughts could Hawk ever allow his mind to consider the one out in the forest who made these Yellow Hairs cringe with fear, could be the banished child he had so skillfully driven from the clan. In fact, during his thinking, she never came to mind. Who was out there he had no idea, but he felt the need to know. As he stood there, staring into the night, a thought crept its way into the forefront of his mind."

'What if I could escape and make my way into the forest and find whoever it is that is bringing war against the Yellow Hairs and join with them; and when they have driven the Yellow Hairs from the land, the clan will think I had a part in it, and then I will once more be looked up to,' "Hawk whispered to himself, a leering smile crossing his lips.

"Looking around, Hawk noticed the nearest guard was

hunkered beneath the limb of a tree on the other side of the camp from where he was standing, drinking from a gourd. Hawk knew from watching the others, by the time he emptied the gourd he would be groggy of mind and sleepy.

"Suddenly, Hawk had a new determination. He would escape! Should he take any of his council with him? he wondered. No, he finally decided. He would go alone and once it was over, he would be the conquering hero and they would be in awe of him and he wouldn't have to share any of the glory.

"Hawk's ego swelled with the thought of being looked up to once again as he watched the guard, now sitting on the ground, the gourd with its strange water lifted to his mouth, some of it dripping from his chin. Hawk wondered what would happen when they found one of the prisoners was missing. Would they come looking for him or were they too afraid of whoever was out in the forest? And what would the other clan members think? Would they think he had slithered away in the darkness, abandoning them?"

'Let them think what they might,' "Hawk said to himself." 'They will sing a different song when I return as their conquering hero.'

"A short time later, Hawk watched as the guard slumped against the tree and the gourd slipped from his fingers. Hawk looked around, searching for the other guards and found they, too, were slumped against trees, sound asleep, while the people of the clan were bunched together in small groups, waiting for the storm to pass.

"Deciding this would be his best chance, Hawk slipped

silently into the forest, the darkness of the night and the rain covering his departure.

"Winter Flower, one of Little Otter's friends and one of the women who had sneaked away from the clan to go see Silent Runner in the past, left the others to go into the forest to be alone and think. She, too, had seen the injured Yellow Hairs and smiled as she remembered the weapons Charlakavos had created and how Silent Runner had become very skillful with them. Could it be Silent Runner that was bringing so much fear to the Yellow Hairs - this young girl of no more than fourteen winters? She was uncanny in the woods and she had seen with her own eyes, Silent Runner running with the wild animals. And hadn't Charlakavos said her daughter, who could not talk like regular people, could somehow speak with the animals. In fact, she could make no noise at all. Winter Flower didn't understand how this could be, and had she not seen it with her own eyes, she, too, would doubt the truth of it.

"Winter Flower was standing under the shelter of a large tree when she heard footsteps and looked in the direction of the noise. There, only a short distance away, she could see Hawk looking all about as though he didn't want to be seen. Winter Flower could not believe her eyes. He was not only a braggart and a liar, but now a coward as well!

"She stepped behind the tree until he passed. Then, as though her legs knew better than her brain, she began to follow him at a safe distance. Was he sneaking away or was he seeking help? But if he was seeking help, who could he be seeking help from? They were not, to the best of her knowledge, friends with any of the other clans, and even if they were, there were no clans who could stand up against the Yellow Hairs. So, what was he up to? she wondered.

"Sven had refrained from consuming as much of the fermented drink as the others. His mind was filled with questions. Who was out in the forest that could conjure up power enough to control wild animals? Plus, whoever it was had knowledge of the bow and arrow, and how to use it. It was difficult for him to believe the animals had been real, not just a vision in the mind of his warriors. But, who could do such a thing? The arrow and wounds to Erick and Adrian's arms were real enough, which was another mystery. His mind was in a whirlwind, trying to understand what was going on. Could there be such a thing as evil spirits, and were they at work here?

"Nonsense, he told himself, spirits are nothing more than old wives tales. This he did believe, yet he could not explain what happened today."

'Tomorrow, I vill take no more chances. I vill load da prisoners onta da ship and vait der at ah safe distance fer Lars and his prisoners ta arrive.' "He was sure evil spirits would not follow him out there.

"Satisfied with his thoughts, Sven picked up a nearly full gourd and lifted it to his lips."

CHAPTER THIRTEEN

-

"During Silent Runner's search for a place to make a camp, Cougar came alongside her and with his mind speak, told her to follow him, which she did without hesitation or questioning where he might be taking her.

"Deep in the forest, Cougar ran under a rock overhang and stopped. Silent Runner ran under the overhang and also stopped. Looking around, she saw several pieces of dry wood off to one side. The area was dry and far away from the Yellow Hairs, who she was sure would not be out searching for her in weather like this.

"Bowing to Cougar, she gave him her thanks for leading her here. Then, with what could only be surprise, she saw a smile cross Cougar's mouth. She had never seen any of the animals smile before and it struck her funny, but she held her laughter. She did not want to embarrass or offend her friend.

"The look on Silent Runner's face did not go unnoticed by Cougar, but he was not offended. She still had a lot to learn about animals. In time, she would come to know that animals had feelings, just like humans do. They cared about their young as well as their pack and would fight to defend them. This human and her mother were different from all the other humans and had become family, but still, she had a lot to learn.

"Silent Runner watched as Cougar bounded from under the overhang and disappeared into the forest.

"As she set about making a fire to not only fix something to eat, but also to keep her warm during the cold night, she could not get the image of Cougar smiling from her mind." 'I think they are not so much different than I am except for our bodies,' "she said to herself as she sat down next to her fire and began to pull food from the small pack she carried.

"Thoughts of her mother and the nice warm cave filled her mind as she ate a small stew made from herbs and wild vegetables, with a few pieces of dried meat thrown in.

"After filling her stomach, she built up the fire to last long into the night, then lay down and closed her eyes. It had been a long day. She had met the Yellow Hairs twice, and been victorious each time, but what about the next time? She knew nothing of warfare and would have to figure things out as she went. What she would do next, she had no idea; only that she had to try her best to rescue her people from their enemy.

"Suddenly she sat up. Her people? Hadn't they banished her and her mother from the clan, no longer wishing to have anything to do with them?

"In all truthfulness, it had been Hawk who had put the thought in their minds.

"But even so, hadn't several of the women sneaked away to

come visit her and her mother? They even learned the sign language she and her mother used. Yes, she thought, these are my people, at least some of them, and I must do all I can to keep them from the kind of life her mother had described in her stories of when she had been one of their captives.

"Silent Runner lay back down, satisfied she was doing the right thing, and closed her eyes. Thunder rumbled across the night sky as the rain continued to fall, but Silent Runner was warm and dry, and snoring lightly.

"Far down the mountainside, Hawk was cursing his misfortune. He was soaked, cold and hungry. He had left on impulse without thinking things through. He had no food, no warm clothing, or water, although the latter was not a concern at this point. For some time now, he had been looking for a place to get in out of the rain where he could get some much-needed rest, but so far, he had seen nothing but trees and no light from the campfire of whoever was out here.

"Taking a short breather, Hawk leaned against a tree and wondered if he had made a mistake leaving during the night and a heavy rain storm. Trying to try find someone in this weather was pure stupidity. Surely, they would be holed up somewhere, snug and dry while he floundered around in the dark. At this point he wasn't even sure he was going in the right direction.

"A short distance away, Winter Flower adjusted her beaver-skin shawl over her head and across her shoulders. She had stopped when Hawk did. Her moccasins were wet, but otherwise, she was dry and only slightly chilled. From her point of view, she could see that Hawk was not doing well, which made her smile. Reaching into the small pouch she always carried, she pulled out a piece of pemmican and took a bite.

"The limb she was standing beneath was heavy with small limbs and leaves, making for the most part, a sheltered place to wait.

"Winter Flower was still a relatively young woman, only twenty-two winters. She had had a mate who went out hunting one day and was never seen again. However, one of the young bucks found a place where a scuffle had taken place and one of his moccasins lay nearby with blood on it. It was decided by Owl that he had been taken by one of the other clans and since they had no children, she would be free to seek another mate, but none so far had approached her except for a few of the older men who only wanted her as someone to cook and clean for them. She knew she was attractive, but already having had a mate made her spoiled as far as the younger men were concerned. They wanted a young, unmated female.

"She knew when morning came, both she and Hawk would be missed and tongues would begin to wag, but she didn't care. Any of the women who knew her, knew she would not leave voluntarily with Hawk. Whatever else they may think she could not concern herself with. Her insides told her Hawk was up to no good and if it involved Silent Runner she wanted to be available to help her friend if she could.

"Hearing a huge grunt, Winter Flower peeked around the side

of the tree and saw Hawk slump down onto the ground in a sitting position with his head between his knees. He seemed to be weeping.

"And indeed, he was. At this point, Hawk felt like the gods had deserted him and he didn't know what to do. If the truth were known, he had never been a good tracker, or warrior. He was big and he was strong and good at wrestling games, and bragging, but he had always had others to do this sort of thing for him. He was a leader, not a worker. Maybe he should turn around and go back before he was missed, he thought. Yes, that is what he should do. Come morning he would find a way to talk to this Sven person even though they didn't speak the same language and he was only a prisoner.

"Resolved with his solution, Hawk gave a grunt and stood up, then wiped his eyes and took a deep breath. All he had to do was backtrack his trail and it would lead him back to the Yellow Hair camp. But as he looked around, everything appeared to be the same to him. It was dark and the rain had washed out any tracks he may have made. After a minute, he made a decision and turned in the opposite direction he had been facing and started walking.

"Not ten feet away, Winter Flower watched as Hawk walked back the way he came, his eyes searching for a trail to follow. Fortunately for Hawk, Winter Flower had blazed a trail by making marks on trees with her knife so she could find her way back if she needed to.

"She watched in silence as Hawk stumbled onto the first mark, which was accidental on his part. He had stopped and leaned his hand against the tree and felt the gouge made by Winter Flower's knife. Leaning in close so he could see, he stood up and looked around, searching to see if he was alone, and when he saw no one, he decided the gods were looking after him, after all.

"Winter Flower watched Hawk venture further into the forest until he disappeared, now full of bravado since he was convinced the gods were on his side.

"What should she do? Winter Flower wondered. Should she go back? Or, should she continue on and hopefully find whoever it was that had put fear into the Yellow Hairs?

"Reaching into the bag at her waist, she pulled out a second piece of pemmican and sat down to think. The rain had slacked up some and the place where she sat was relatively dry.

"What if it wasn't Silent Runner out there? What if it was disgruntled Yellow Hairs, or someone else? Her mind was filled with what ifs. Finally, when she had eaten the last bite of the pemmican, she stood up and plucked a large, wide leaf from the tree and held it up so it would catch some rainwater, and when it was full, she drank. She had to do this several times to get her fill, but by the time she'd quenched her thirst, she had made a decision. She would wait until morning when she could see, then make her way up the mountain in search of whoever was raging war against the Yellow Hairs.

"Whatever or whoever was out there had to be better than being a slave or comfort for the Yellow Hair warriors.

CHAPTER FOURTEEN

-

"Morning came, clear and clean smelling. A blue-jay landed on Silent Runner's toe and was singing to her when her eyes opened and she smiled."

'Good morning to you, too,' "she said to the blue-jay, with her mind speak. He flapped his wings twice before lifting off her foot and heading back out into the sunshine.

"The coals and embers from last night's fire were smoldering in the small fire pit and Silent Runner added more fuel, then hung a tightly woven pot near the flames, but not directly over them. She filled the pot with water and dropped in some herbs and spices and a few pieces of dried meat. In a large gourd, she warmed water for washing and when it was warm, she washed herself, then braided her long hair into a ponytail so it wouldn't tangle in the brush or get caught on tree limbs in case she should need to move quickly.

"After she'd bathed and eaten, she cleaned up her camp and took a leafy branch and wiped out any sign of her being there before venturing back down the mountain in search of the Yellow Hairs.

"She had gone no more than a mile when her senses told her someone was headed in her direction. She looked around for a place of concealment where she could defend herself.

"What she found was a space between two boulders that would allow her to see who was coming up the mountain, without them seeing her. She slid into her hiding place and drew an arrow from the deerskin quiver that hung from her shoulder, and notched it on her bowstring.

"She was tense, ready to let the arrow fly when her mind heard Wolf speak to her. She looked behind her and saw him standing there." 'Put your weapon away, it is not the enemy, but a friend,' "Wolf told her.

"Silent Runner returned the arrow to the quiver and waited, still hidden behind the boulder.

"She didn't have to wait long when to her surprise, she saw Winter Flower come into view. She was walking with her head down; seeming to be looking for tracks, but whose, Silent Runner wasn't sure.

"She started to run out and greet her friend, but checked herself as an idea flashed in her brain. She turned and looked at Wolf and sent him a message with her mind speak.

"Winter Flower was indeed searching for a track of some kind and not paying attention to her surroundings, when suddenly she heard a growl and looked up. No more than ten feet in front of her stood the biggest and meanest looking wolf she'd ever seen. The fur on his back was standing on end and his mouth was open, slobbers dripping from his chin. His sharp teeth looked ready to tear her flesh to pieces, and the loud growling coming from deep in his chest caused Winter Flower's body to go rigid. It was all she could do to keep from screaming. Her breath was coming in ragged gulps. Her heart was racing. She wanted to turn and run, but instead, she fainted.

"Winter Flower felt something wet and rough against her face and opened her eyes and saw the giant wolf was licking her face. She started to scream when a hand clamped over her mouth and she found herself looking directly into the steel blue eyes of Silent Runner.

"She gave a sigh and slumped back down as the giant wolf stepped back and sat down on his haunches, wagging his tail."

'I thought I was going to be eaten alive,' "Winter Flower said when at last she'd regained her composure enough to speak.

"Knowing Winter Flower could use the hand speak, Silent Runner apologized for scaring her and told her it was her idea of a joke."

'Well you almost scared me to death,' "Winter Flower said as she sat up and smiled." 'But you are forgiven,' "she giggled, getting to her feet."

'What are you doing up here? Did you run away from the Yellow Hairs?' "Silent Runner asked, knowing it was a silly question."

'I came looking for you. I knew you were the only one with skill enough to use their kind of weapons against them, and the only one who even had those kinds of weapons.'

"She went on to tell about seeing Hawk sneak away and following him, then when he went back, she decided to come in search of Silent Runner."

'I want to help. What can I do?' "Winter Flower asked."

'I'm not sure,' "Silent Runner responded." 'But right now, I need to know where their camp is, how many warriors they have and how many people they have taken.'

"Winter Flower thought for a minute, then said," 'There are at least twenty or more of the yellow haired warriors in the camp right now, but close to that many have gone off to gather more prisoners from other clans. We are the only clan they have taken as prisoners so far, but as I said, there are warriors out collecting more. How soon they will come back? I do not know.'

'Have you eaten since leaving the camp?' "Silent Runner asked. She was anxious to be on her way, but as she well knew, you cannot travel well on an empty stomach.

"Winter Flower smiled and withdrew a piece of pemmican from her pouch.

"Silent Runner nodded her head and said," 'Good, that will do for now. Let us be on our way. I need you to lead me to their camp.'

"Without a word, Winter Flower turned and headed back down the trail, not considering what Sven was doing at that very moment.

"Sven had slept badly. He kept having dreams about a phantom ghost shooting arrows into his chest and by the time the sun was trying to make its way over the horizon, he was up and shouting orders to move the prisoners aboard his ship.

"When Erick asked why he was not waiting for Lars and the

others, Sven felt the fear he'd had in the night rise in him, but did his best to control it and took Erick to the side so the prisoners or his men wouldn't hear."

'Did ya see da vons dat shot arrows at ya?' "Sven asked in a low voice, his bleary eyes constantly scanning the forest for any unusual movement."

'No, my lord,' "Erick said." 'Da arrows yust came flying out of da air. Vee saw no von but da vild animals dat ver snarlin' and growlin' at us.'

'And did dat not seem strange ta ya?' "Sven asked."

'Ya. It vas like vee ver fightin' spirits. And like Adrian said, ya cannot fight spirits. Since vee could see no von ta fight, vee came back ta da safety of our camp.'

"Sven nodded his head." 'But is da camp safe from being attacked by da spirits? If dat's vat it vas. I do not believe in spirits, myself, but I have ta tink of da safety of da men. During da night, I decided da safest place ta fight from vould be from da ship. Der, vee can defend ourselves from vatever it may be, human or spirit.'

"After thinking about it for a moment, Erick saw the wisdom in his leader's thinking and began to shout at the men to gather the prisoners together and load them onto the ship.

"Because of their night of drinking, the men were slow to follow orders, which caused Sven to yell at Erick, who in turn yelled at the men, causing even more confusion.

"Hawk had made it back to the clan unseen and when he

understood what the Yellow Hairs were doing, he approached Erick and tried to speak to him and got knocked down and beaten for his effort, then grabbed by the hair on his head and dragged to the front of where they were lining up the prisoners. He was dropped unceremoniously onto the ground.

"Hawk was seething with anger and shame. He had been humiliated in front of the clan and knew inside they were laughing at him. One of his followers reached down and tried to help Hawk to his feet, but he shook off his hand and stood up on his own. Hawk glared at the rest of the clan, silently daring them to laugh or say something.

"The people of the clan could see Hawk's anger and knew it would not take much for him to explode and do something stupid, so they wisely kept quiet. A large portion of them averted their eyes toward the ground.

"Erick took in a big gulp of air as his eyes scanned the woods. He'd done as he'd been ordered and was, hisself, anxious to go aboard the ship. The thought of fighting spirits put his nerves on edge. He had not seen anyone or anything except the arrows appearing out of nowhere, which amounted to spirits, for if it had been humans, they would have seen them, he concluded. Even the pinecones seemed to come from nowhere, yet they seemed to come from everywhere."

'Da prisoners are ready ta board da long boats, my lord. Vat are yer orders?' "Erick asked of Sven.

"Sven looked around, searching the forest, his nerves even

more tense than earlier."

'I vill take four men and go aboard and prepare fer da prisoners. Ven vee are ready, I vill have von of da men vave ah blue flag and den ya can put da prisoners in da long boats and bring dem out ta da ship,' "Sven told his second in command.

"Erick could see the fear in his lordship's face and was puzzled. Never before could he remember seeing Sven afraid.

"Erick nodded his head, hoping Sven would not take long." 'As ya vish, my lord.'

"Erick watched as his leader rushed out to one of the small boats, accompanied by four of their best warriors and headed for the ship.

"Turning, Erick barked orders for his men to get the prisoners lined up and ready to load into the remaining long boats.

"Winter Flower and Silent Runner were making their way down the mountainside when Cougar came up alongside Silent Runner and said in his mind speak," 'You must hurry. They are preparing to take your people out onto the water where the floating things sit bobbing up and down on the water.'

"Since Silent Runner had never seen a ship and was confused by Cougar's statement.

"She turned to Winter Flower and said," 'Cougar said the Yellow Hairs are moving the people out onto things that float on the water. How can that be? Do they have so many floating things they can carry them all?'

"Winter Flower thought for a moment before responding."

'The yellow haired warriors came across the big water in three large things they call, ships. They are huge wooden things that float on the water. How they work I do not know, but somehow they can make them go wherever they want.'

'And these, ships, as you call them, are large enough to hold everyone in the clan?'

"Silent Runner was trying to imagine in her mind something large enough to hold that many people, and was having difficulty picturing it."

'We must hurry, then,' "she said with quick movements of her hands, just before they broke into a run.

"Once aboard his ship, Sven's anxiety began to subside and the first thing he did was to go to his cabin and pour himself a large mug of fermented water. It burned all the way down his throat and into his stomach, but even so, he felt himself begin to relax.

"He walked over and peered through a porthole window. From there, he could see the prisoners and the rest of his men. They were standing on the beach, awaiting his order to come out to the ship, but for some reason, Sven hesitated in sending the order.

"The ship was ready and the hold where the prisoners would be taken was empty. He knew of no reason for him to not send the signal, but his mind was in a quandary."

'If I bring da prisoners out ta da ship, vill dat anger da spirits even more?' "he asked himself."

'Can spirits leave da land? Can dey attack my ship? If I cannot see da spirits, how can I fight them?' "he pondered." 'If I do nuthing and turn da prisoners loose, vill da spirits be appeased? And vat of da udders? Vill da spirits fight fer dem too? And my men, vat vill happen ta them?' "Sven wondered, drinking another mug of the strong liquid.

"Sven's inability to decide what to do was actually good for Silent Runner and Winter Flower, giving them time to reach the camp before the prisoners were loaded into the long boats.

"In fact, while Sven was hiding aboard his ship, Winter Flower and Silent Runner came to a place just beyond the Yellow Hair's camp and stopped to watch and observe the scene below.

"Almost instantly, Silent Runner realized the Yellow Hairs were afraid. They seemed very nervous, constantly scanning the forest as though they expected an army to attack them at any moment.

"Letting her eyes wander out beyond the land, Silent Runner stared in wonderment. She had never seen the ocean before and was, at least for a moment, mesmerized. Nor had she ever seen a ship and she shook her head. She had seen limbs floating on the river and in ponds, but never anything like this. There were three of the large floating things, she noted."

'Are those the ships, as you called them, the things the Yellow Hairs came in?'

"Winter Flower nodded her head, yes."

'They came across the big water in them and plan to take their prisoners back in them.'

"Silent Runner remembered something her mother had said about seeing the floating things when she had been captured, but had escaped before being loaded onto one of them."

'What can we do?' "Winter Flower asked.

"Silent Runner could swim and knew fish swam in the ponds and rivers, for she had captured many of them. She had grown to like fresh cooked fish, but what kind of creatures swam in the big water? Could she communicate with them? she wondered. She'd never tried to mind talk to the fish in the rivers and ponds and didn't know if she could.

"As she looked upon the scene below her, a plan began to develop in her mind and she turned to Cougar and began to reveal her plan to him through mind speak, and when she'd finished - without a sound, Cougar turned and ran off into the forest.

"Winter Flower watched with amazement as her friend, the one the clan had banished as a baby because she was different, was now communicating with a wild animal, and to the best of her guessing, a plan to save them from the Yellow Hairs.

"If she was successful, what would they think of her then? Would they appreciate what she had done or look at her like evil spirits possessed her and continue to shun her?

"When they were alone again, Winter Flower looked at Silent Runner and asked," 'Do you have a plan to save them?' "indicating with her head, the people down below, waiting to be loaded aboard the floating thing and a life of slavery.

"Silent Runner smiled and said with her hands moving in the hand speak," 'Yes, and I will need your help.'

'I will do whatever I can,' "Winter Flower said." 'But what is it you want me to do?'

'When the time comes, you must be quick for we will not have much time.'

CHAPTER FIFTEEN

-

"Erick paced up and down the beach, waiting and watching for the sign telling him to bring the prisoners aboard the ship."

'Vat is he vaiting on?' "Erick asked aloud.

"Looking over his shoulder for the twentieth time in the past hour, to make sure they weren't being attacked by evil spirits, he sighed. Everything seemed peaceful, but that didn't mean they were safe. He knew the spirits could strike at any time. He also noticed his men glancing over their shoulders, studying the forest; many of them with a hand on their sword or battle-axe, ready to fight their unseen foe should they need to.

"Aboard the ship, Sven continued to partake of the strong liquid which was giving him false hope and courage."

'Vhy should I fear spirits ven I do not believe in der existence?' "he asked himself." 'I am Sven, mightiest of all da varriors in my country. No von has ever defeated me in battle. I am feared by all men, so vhy should I let a few spirits scare me?'

"Sven had just downed the last of the courage giving liquid in the jug and started for the passageway that would take him back up on deck when he heard the mournful howling of what sounded like a thousand wolves coming from the beach.

"He turned and ran to the porthole window and pressed his face against the glass. He looked toward the shore. He saw nothing but his men standing, weapons in their hands, staring at the forest. Was it really wolves howling, or was it the spirits howling, making them believe it was wolves?

"By now, the strong liquid was affecting both his thinking and his movement. Staggering, he made his way to the deck and saw the four warriors he'd brought with him, standing next to the railing with arrows strung on their bowstrings, searching for something to shoot at.

"With a great show of bravado, Sven drew his sword and joined his men at the railing and was surprised to see fear in their eyes. These were fearless men who were the best of his men; warriors each of them, yet, there they stood, staring wide eyed at the shore and the water between them, searching for an unseen enemy."

'Ya heard dem, my lord?' "Larson, a very large warrior who had come through many battles, unscathed, asked."

'I did. But I see no enemy,' "Sven said, trying his best to sound sober."

'I fear it is da evil spirits vee face, and I da not know how ta fight someting I cannot see,' "Larson said, hoping Sven would have an answer.

"For the first time Sven could remember, he had no answer. His mind was too confused by the fermented brew. Plus, he didn't know whether he now believed in spirits or not? He had never believed in them before, but now, he was no longer sure.

"Somehow, he heard himself saying," 'Vee shall vait and vatch. So far vee have only heard da howling of da volves and eerie as dey sound, howling cannot hurt us. I tink whoever is out der in da voods, maybe dey are tryin' ta scare us inta runnin'. If and ven vee see da enemy, den vee vill fight,' "Sven said, sounding braver than he felt."

'Shouldn't vee go ashore ta help Erick?' "Larson asked.

"Sven did not want to go ashore and subject himself to whatever was there and he was about to say so when another chorus of loud snarls, growls and howling came rushing across the water causing all five of them to jump.

"They rushed to the starboard side of the ship and stared in the direction of the sounds.

Everyone on shore, including the prisoners, had drawn together as if to help protect one another.

"Sven looked past the men and women on the beach and let his eyes search the woods and what he saw caused him to cringe. There, just at the edge of the woods, standing side by side were, wolves, mountain lions, bears, bobcats, and even giant elk; all staring as though they were famished and wanting to feast on the flesh of his men.

"At this point the Yellow Hairs forgot about the prisoners and stood side by side with their weapons drawn, afraid, yet ready to fight for their lives. Some of them were saying a prayer to whichever god they believed in for they thought they might die here on this sandy shore so far from home.

"Silent Runner stood back, just inside the tree line so she would not be seen. She had told Winter Flower to ease back into the camp and tell at least ten people to follow her and she would help them escape into the woods.

"She watched as Winter Flower moved among the prisoners, whispering to a selected few, mostly women, who moved to a place close to the woods and waited, trying hard to not attract attention as they whispered among themselves, wondering if they were doing the right thing. Two of the older women were apprehensive, but agreed to go. Even death would be better than what lay ahead of them. The young men Winter Flower asked to escape with them were brave and she felt they would help protect them if it came to a fight for their lives.

"When Winter Flower was ready, she looked in the direction where Silent Runner was hiding and nodded her head.

"Silent Runner closed her eyes and sent a mind speak message to her friends, and suddenly the animals came a short distance farther out of the woods, snarling and growling, causing the Yellow Hair guards to step backwards and come to the ready with their weapons.

"The animals stopped far enough away so the Yellow Hairs wouldn't be forced to attack them, yet close enough to be threatening.

"While the Yellow Hairs were concentrating on the wild animals facing them, suddenly, without warning, the air was filled with the fluttering of wings and the screech of both hawks and eagles, along with crows and several other smaller birds who swooped down on the guards, pecking at them, beating them with their wings and drawing blood from some of them with their sharp beaks and talons.

"While the guards were busy defending themselves against the birds, Winter Flower and the people she'd selected, sneaked quietly into the forest.

"Silent Runner thought it would be easier, while the guards were preoccupied with the animals surrounding the camp and the birds causing havoc, if they took only a few at a time. That way they wouldn't be readily missed when the attack was over and hopefully they would be far away before anyone noticed some of them were gone.

"When Winter Flower brought the ten people to the place in the woods where Silent Runner was waiting, they all stopped, their eyes wide at the sight of her, dressed as a warrior with weapons like those of the Yellow Hairs hanging on her shoulders."

'What evil is this?' "one of the two older women asked, since she had not been one of the women who had visited Silent Runner and her mother in the past and still thought of Silent Runner and her mother as possessed by evil spirits.

"She and another older woman were ready to turn and go back, but Winter Flower and the other women stepped in front of them and quickly explained that Silent Runner was not under the influence of evil spirits but born with special powers and was here to help them escape their fate at the hands of the Yellow Hairs.

"Although they were not totally convinced, they relinquished somewhat and they had to admit she did not seem threatening, standing there, smiling at them. They liked the idea of a female being a warrior, but it would take some getting used to.

"Suddenly, all of them except Winter Flower stepped back, stifling the screams in their throats as Cougar came running up and stopped next to Silent Runner.

"With eyes wide and astonished looks on their faces, they watched as Silent Runner reached down and stroked Cougar on the neck and scratched his ears, hearing the purring sound coming from deep in his chest.

"Silent Runner stared down at the big cat as though they were conversing, then Cougar turned and ran back into the forest.

"Silent Runner made her hand talk to Wild Flower, who translated and told them it was time to go. The animals would circle around and block the guards from following them until they were a safe distance away.

"All were astonished with Silent Runner's relationship with a cougar and were even more astounded to learn that she was able to communicate with the wild animals. They also looked at Winter Flower suspiciously because of her ability to understand Silent Runner's hand talk. Was there no end to the strange things they must get used to?

"Before Winter Flower could offer an explanation, Silent Runner turned and led them up the mountainside to the place she had been staying and told Winter Flower to tell them there was food and shelter here and that she and Winter Flower would return as soon as they could with more of their friends.

"The small group of people who had been rescued were both confused and scared. What if the Yellow Hairs came and found them? Or, what if the Yellow Hairs captured Silent Runner and Winter Flower – what would they do then? Where could they go and not have to worry about the Yellow Hairs finding them?

"Even though they had been assured this would not happen, they huddled together and watched as Silent Runner and Winter Flower disappeared into the forest. After a while, they turned and set about lighting a fire and preparing a much-needed meal. There was nothing more they could do but watch and wait.

"One of the young males who came with them, volunteered to climb a tree and watch for the enemy, hoping they were too busy with the animals to come looking for them.

CHAPTER SIXTEEN

-

"Sven had been watching with his long glass and saw the small bunch of women and two young braves sneak into the forest and then watched in astonishment as the wild animals filled the area so the prisoners couldn't be followed and pointed it out to Liam and the other three standing safely on the deck of his ship."

'How can dis be?' "Liam wanted to know. 'Vhy are dey not afraid of da wild animals and vhy do da animals protect dem?'

"By now, this whole event had sobered Sven, and his mind was racing in several directions." 'Da animals are not acting on their own and I da not believe der are evil spirits guiding them. No, dey are being controlled by somevon strong of mind dat has power ober dem. Ya, dat is vat I believe,' "Sven said, shaking his head up and down.

"Loud cries from the beach caused Sven and his men to turn and look at the shore. The animals and birds were gone and Erick was yelling for permission to bring the prisoners on board the ship."

'No!' "Sven screamed." 'Vee are coming ashore. Some of the prisoners have escaped and I vant dem back!'

"And with that, Sven and his four men went over the side and climbed down the rope ladder and got into the longboat tied to the side. In just a few minutes, they were back on the beach with a confused Erick waiting on his leader."

'I counted and der are eleven missing,' "Erick yelled with a concerned look on his face as they approached." 'How can ya know dis?' "Erick asked as Sven and his men walked up to them."

'I saw dem tru my long glass vile you ver defending yerselves against da birds. Dat is ven dey left and da animals filled da area so ya could not chase dem.'

"Erick shook his head in wonderment. It was more than he could comprehend. This land was haunted and he wanted no more of it. He wanted to take what prisoners they had and leave and never come back, and expressed his view to Sven.

"Sven could understand Erick's feelings and the feelings of all of them, but somehow he must convince them it was not evil spirits doing this and the land was not haunted. How he was going to accomplish this would not be done by him just saying it was so, no, it must be done by finding and facing down whoever it was that had such power over the animals and birds.

"While Sven was trying to devise a plan to track down and get back the prisoners he'd lost, the other group of Yellow Hairs, led by a huge, red headed warrior by the name of Lars, who was also called, Lars the Terrible because of his bad temper and his fighting abilities, had already overpowered two other clans and was camped near a third clan.

"Lars smiled as he stood at the top of the rise overlooking the area where the third clan sat, watching as the unsuspecting people went about fixing their evening meal."

'By dis time tomorrow, I vill have more dan ah hundred prisoners ta take back ta da homeland. Far more dan Sven, I betcha.'

"Even though Sven was his leader, Lars was not, and never would be, a follower of Sven. Lars knew Sven to be the people's choice for leader of the raids, but he was weak when it came right down to it. And when this trip was over and he proved he was the stronger warrior, and had taken more prisoners, they would elect him leader of the next raid and someday, leader of the great and mighty Fens, the greatest fighting force in the entire world. He might even choose Erick to be his second in command or... he might have to do away with him, he had not yet decided.

"Lars turned and walked back down the hill, his plan for the next morning churning in his mind. There was one way to fight and one way only, his way, which meant, attack your enemy when they least expected it with superior forces – and if you didn't have superior forces, make them believe you did.

"The men who followed Lars had been hand-picked. They knew his way of warfare and followed his orders without question. And because of this, they had had many victories - more than any of the other hunting parties.

"Sven knew of Lars' hatred of him but didn't care. This would be his last trip in search of slaves and he cared not a whit if Lars became the new commander. His only desire at the moment was to get his prisoners back and hopefully prove to his men there were no evil spirits to fight, just people like themselves. At least that's what he hoped.

"From their hiding place among the trees, Silent Runner and Winter Flower watched as Erick convinced Sven to load what prisoners they had aboard the ship so whoever was stealing them could steal no more of them while they were off seeking the ones who had escaped. And when they began loading the prisoners into boats and taking them out to the ship, Silent Runner shook her head. What was she to do now? At first, she thought it would be easy with the help of the animals, but what was she to do now with them out on the water on that big floating thing called a ship?

"Winter Flower sighed with despair, then whispered in Silent Runner's ear," 'We have lost them. There is no longer any hope of saving them.'

"Silent Runner was not about to give up. She would watch and wait, which is exactly what she did. She watched the small flotations carry the people out to the big ship and watched as they climbed up the rope ladder hanging on the side and then disappeared into the belly of the huge floating thing like being swallowed by a large animal.

"Thinking he would need as many men as he could muster, Sven left only three men to guard the prisoners aboard the ship, which in his mind would be more than enough since the prisoners were confined in the lower part of the ship, behind a locked door.

"Silent Runner watched as Sven and his men marched into the forest in search of the prisoners who had escaped.

"After they had gone, she hand talked to Winter Flower, revealing a plan she had come up with."

'That is very clever,' "Winter Flower said," 'but be careful, there are still three of them guarding their floating thing they call a ship.'

"A few minutes later Silent Runner noticed only one man walking about on the deck of the floating thing where the prisoners were held and nodded her head. She looked at Winter Flower and said with her hands," 'It is time.'

"Leaving Winter Flower, Silent Runner circled around until she was out of sight when she left the forest and eased into the water. She had learned to swim in the rivers and the ponds, but had never been in salt water and although it felt different against her skin, it was easier to swim in, even with all her weapons.

"Winter Flower watched with fascination as Silent Runner swam up to the bow of the big ship and made her way around to the net. The guard was sitting on a barrel in a relaxed position, looking at the shore and not expecting anyone to be coming aboard. And when Silent Runner climbed over the rail and stood facing him, he was momentarily stunned.

"He could tell it was a female, but she was dressed like a warrior. He opened his mouth to call out to the other two guards who were down below, sleeping, but no sound came out. An arrow had pierced his windpipe. He felt his legs grow weak, then nothing.

"Silent Runner dragged his body to the far side of the ship and dumped it over the side, then stood in awe as large fish looking creatures with razor teeth appeared and quickly devoured the dead guard. She looked at the sky and thanked the gods for not letting them eat her, not realizing it was the warrior's blood that had attracted them.

"Looking around, Silent Runner saw the opening that led below and with great caution, crept down the stairs. Behind two of the doors she heard snoring and continued on down a second set of stairs and there, deep inside the floating thing, she found the people. They were huddled together in fear. And when she stepped into the light in front of the locked door, they gasped at the sight of her. She looked like a female Yellow Hair warrior and only a few of them actually recognized her in the dim light.

"She tried the door but it wouldn't open and she didn't know what to do. She had never seen a locked door before. Finally, one of the women ventured toward her and pointed to the opening where the key went and made gestures with her hands.

"Silent Runner nodded and put her finger against her lips, indicating that they make no noise, then turned and went back up the stairs. At one of the doors where she heard loud snoring, she found a latch and pushed on it and the door opened easily. Inside she saw a man laying on his back, his mouth open, emitting the loud noise. She giggled to herself, then drawing her knife, she eased over to his side and touched his shoulder.

"His eyes fluttered open and in the semi darkness took a moment to realize a woman dressed as a warrior was standing next to him with a knife in her hand. He looked at her for a moment then lunged at her, grabbing for the hand that held the knife, but got only air for his effort. And the next thing he knew, one of his arms was pinned behind him and he felt the edge of the knife pressed against his throat.

"He was shoved into a chair and saw the woman motioning with her hands, indicating she wanted him to unlock the door where the prisoners were kept.

"He chuckled and said, shaking his head and pointing toward the door," 'You got da vrong von. I don't have da key. Carl does and he von't be so easy ta sneak up on.'

"And with that, he lunged again for the hand holding the knife and this time grabbed her by the arm and swung her around. They wrestled around the cabin with the guard finding her much stronger than he'd first thought. Jerking on her arm, they both went stumbling over a small chest sitting on the floor, and as they fell he felt something sharp penetrate his stomach.

"Silent Runner tried to jerk her hand out of the guards' grip, but he was stronger and jerked her arm back - and in doing so, drove the knife into his stomach. His eyes went wide and he let out a single scream before he fell to the floor, dead.

"Silent Runner had barely gotten to her feet when Carl, a man twice the size of the one she'd just been fighting with, came charging through the door, shouting," 'Vot's goin' on in here? Can't ah man get...'

"Carl stopped when he saw Silent Runner standing over his friend with a bloody knife in her hand. He could see from the way his friend lay there that he was dead."

'Vot is dis? Vot are ya doin' here? And vot have ya done vit my friend?'

"Silent Runner saw a ring of metal keys hanging from his waist and figured those must be the things she needed to open the door. She pointed at them and then herself and held out her hand.

"Carl watched with fascination as this wisp of a girl ordered him to turn over his keys to her, then with a wide grin and a motion of his hands, he said," 'Come and get dem.'

"Without taking her eyes off the man, she reached down and wiped the blood off the blade of her knife then put it back in its sheath; then once again, held out her hand.

"Already, Carl was tired of the game and strode toward her." 'Ye'll be beggin' fer mercy ven I get tru vit ya.'

"Instead of backing away like Carl thought she would, Silent Runner stepped toward him and then dropped into a crouch and kicked out her leg, smashing it against his shin.

"He let out a yelp and felt himself falling forward. Unconsciously he threw his arms out in front of him to break his fall but felt his other leg being jerked out from under him and the last thing he saw was the edge of the chest, then a sharp pain above his left eye, and then, nothing.

"Silent Runner wasted no time. Both men were dead. She had now killed three men and hated the thought of what she'd done. She had not intentionally killed either one of these men, only the one up on the top. Bending down, she grabbed the key ring and raced back down the stairs, and when she got to the door, she saw Hawk standing there with his hand reaching through the bars of their prison.

"Silent Runner stopped just out of his reach and shook her head, no, then motioned for him to step back.

"Seething with anger, Hawk reached again, saying," 'Give me the keys, girl!'

"But Silent Runner motioned again for him to step back. He did not like taking orders, especially from this whelp he had gotten banished from the clan. He felt humiliated, but common sense overrode his anger and he relinquished his position and stepped back.

"One of the younger women who had been to see Silent Runner and her mother had been learning to read and understand the sign language. She stepped forward and smiled at Silent Runner.

"As she took Hawk's place next to the barred door, she began to make gestures with her hands and in return, Silent Runner answered her. The clans people watched in amazement, with several gasps and a lot of whispering.

"Silent Runner smiled to herself as she stuck the key into the lock and turned it and after the door was open, she worked the mechanism several times, marveling at it.

"Once she had them all on deck, she found there were three young women who could use the silent hand talk and told them what she wanted them to do, and when they had relayed her message, several of the women, along with some of the warriors shook their heads, no, indicating they had never learned to swim.

"Silent Runner looked over the side of the ship but there were no small boats tied to the side; they were all on the beach, which ruled out taking them ashore in one of the small floating things. Next, she looked around and found several things that would float; and after finding six strong looking warriors who said they were good swimmers, she cut pieces of rope and tied them to the flotations, then gave them to the strong swimmers. The idea was for the ones who could not swim to hang onto the flotations while the strong swimmers towed them the short distance to the beach.

"At first, they rebelled even getting into the water - but they were more afraid of being left behind than the possibility of drowning, so they did as they were told.

"Before letting any of the prisoners leave the ship, Silent Runner climbed one of the tall pole like trees without limbs that stood on the flat part of the ship, so she could get a good look at the other two ships and gave a sigh of relief when she saw no Yellow Hair guards aboard.

"As she was climbing down, an idea wormed its way into her brain and by the time she was once again back down on the flat part of the ship, it had become a full-blown plan.

"Hurriedly, Silent Runner helped the prisoners over the side and watched them slip into the water and head for the beach. When they were close to the beach and began to walk out of the water on their own, she turned and went down below.

"In the big cabin she found a lantern burning brightly and smiled. This would do nicely she decided. Looking around, she found three more and when they were all lit, she lifted one and threw it at the bed.

"Immediately the bed began to burn, its flames reaching out to other parts of the room.

"Wasting no time, Silent Runner raced through the lower quarters of the ship, tossing the lit lanterns into various rooms, hearing them burst and the whoosh as the interiors began to burn, and then she sprinted up onto the flat part and fresh air.

"Without waiting, she dove over the side and swam to the nearest ship and climbed up the net hanging on the side. Once aboard, she repeated what she'd done on the other ship, then jumped into the water and began swimming for the shore.

"Once she was on land again, she turned and looked back out across the water. Both ships were ablaze, two huge columns of black smoke climbed into the sky. In a very short time they would be burned so badly they could never be used again and what was left, would disappear below the surface of the water. She left the third ship unharmed on purpose so the Yellow Hairs would have something to carry them back to where they came from, that is if she could convince them it would be unsafe for them to stay here.

"Turning, Silent Runner nodded to Winter Flower and headed into the forest. It would not be long before the Yellow Hairs saw the large cloud of smoke and came running back. She and the others needed to be far away by the time they arrived. When they saw two of their floating things burning, they would be very angry.

"Silent Runner smiled to herself. Except for the killing of three of them, she was proud of what she had accomplished so far.

She hoped the people of the clan would look at her differently now. She hoped they wouldn't think of her as an evil thing, but someone no different than they were.

"What she didn't realize was that after seeing her talking with her hands, being friendly with wild animals and dressed as a warrior and using warrior's weapons, they were all the more convinced she was possessed. No ordinary woman they had ever known of could do any of those things.

CHAPTER SEVENTEEN

-

"Sven was searching for human footprints when one of his men touched him lightly on the shoulder, and when he turned, the warrior pointed at the sky.

"It took only a moment before Sven began running back down the trail, his anger rising with each footstep for his stupidity. He had miscalculated his foes thinking and abilities, and had been made to look the fool because of it, and he didn't like it. Wild animals did not set fires. Someone wanted him gone so they could sneak in like the cowards they were and destroy his ships. His only hope was that they had not burned them all. A new ship would take at least a year to build, and longer if they were harassed by this enemy who stayed hidden and struck when he wasn't there to defend his property.

"Sven and his men were not the only ones to see the sky turning black with smoke from the pitch used to seal the seams of the ships. Lars and his men had just raided another clan and were marching them back to the holding area where other prisoners awaited their fate. When the smell of smoke reached his nostrils, he lifted his head and saw the sky filling up with black smoke and knew immediately where the smoke was coming from. He quickly left a dozen men to bring the prisoners down to the beach, while he and the rest ran back down the mountain.

"Lars couldn't fathom in his mind what might have happened. At least one of their ships was on fire, of that he was certain. Had some drunken guard fallen asleep and caused the fire? he wondered. Never in his mind did he think there might be an imposing force against them. None of these illiterate savages would have the nerve to even try, so it had to be one of their own. If only one ship was gone, they could still go back victorious; a little cramped, but victorious. He just hoped the other two ships were far enough away that flames or wind driven sparks had not been carried the distance and set them on fire, also.

"Sven and his men ran out onto the beach in time to see what was left of two of his ships, disappear slowly into the bay with loud hissing sounds as the burning wood met the water.

"Turning to one of his sergeants, he ordered him and two men to go aboard the last remaining ship and search it from top to bottom." 'If ya find somebody, bring'um ta me!' "he said." 'Vee vill let dem feel vat fire really feels like ven vee burn dem at da stake in front of vatever might be vatchin' from da forest.'

"Giving quick salutes, the three warriors rushed down to the boats and rowed out to the last remaining ship.

"Lars and his men came running onto the beach and stopped when they saw only one ship still floating in the bay.

"Striding up to Sven he looked down at the shorter man and asked," 'Vat happened? Did von of yer drunken louts cause dis?'

"Sven was instantly angered and could feel the heat rising within him. He took a deep breath and as calmly as he could, explained the recent events." 'So, it musta been von of vatever is out der dat did dis ven vee ver out lookin' fer dem.'

'Ya musta left guards. Vat happened ta dem?' "Lars asked, rolling his eyes.

"Sven shook his head." 'I vould not know. Vatever it vas musta overpowered dem and killed dem, cause I know fer sure dey vould not give up da ships vitout ah fight.'

'Dis makes no sense,' "Lars said." 'Dese people are not varriors. Dey are cowards and know nothing about varfare. How many varriors do dey have?'

"Again, Sven shook his head." 'I vould not know dat eiter. Vee have seen no von, only da animals I told ya about. I tink vatever it is can somehow control da animals and stays in hiding until vee go out lookin' fer dem, den comes in ta raise havoc vit us.'

"Lars stared at the sky for a long moment, then turned back to Sven." 'Ya make no sense, man. People cannot control vild animals. It has ta be evil spirits vat tricked ya inta tinkin' ya vas seein' vild animals.'

'And so, ya now believe in evil spirits, Lars? Ya never did before as I recall,' "Sven said with a smirk on his lips."

'Ta tell ya da truth, I don't know vat ta believe right now. I say vee post some guards ta watch da last ship and vee go hunt down dese evil spirits. I vant ta see dem face ta face. I vant ta see if dey can eat hard steel, cause I don't tink spirits can do vat has been done here taday,' "Lars said, patting the sword at his side.

"When the three men Sven sent to check on the last remaining ship returned and told them the ship was unharmed, five of Lars' men and five of Sven's men rowed out to stand guard on the last ship."

'Der vill be no drinkin' or sleepin', or ya vill deal vit me,' "Lars told them."

'And dat goes fer me, too,' "Sven said, shaking his axe at them." 'Dat ship is our only vay home. So, if ya don't vant ta be left ashore ta face da evil spirits, you'd better die before ya let anythin' happen ta dat ship.'

"The men chosen to stay behind snapped to attention and drew their fists across their chests in a salute, signaling they would do as they were told.

"Satisfied, Lars and Sven watched as the ones chosen rowed out to the last ship and climbed aboard. Then, with the other prisoners being guarded by ten of their warriors, they began to scout the area, looking for footprints to follow.

"By now, the sun was at its highest point and shining brightly and it wasn't long before one of the warriors found the tracks the prisoners had made when they rushed into the forest.

"Looking down at the footprints of the prisoners, Lars proclaimed," 'If da savages are not afraid of da evil spirits den vhy should vee be afraid of dem?'

"This was a revelation none of them had considered and there was considerable talking among each other.

"Lars beamed with pride at being the one to think of this and looked over to see Sven's reaction, who just shrugged his shoulders and then headed into the woods, following the large group of tracks." 'Maybe dey are not evil spirits ta da savages. Maybe dey are protective spirits fer dem,' "he muttered to himself.

"While the rest might think the way Lars did, Sven held his suspicions to himself, waiting to see when and if they caught up to whoever or whatever was out there."

CHAPTER EIGHTEEN

-

Singing Bird looked around and saw the sun was headed toward the western side of the valley. She'd been so absorbed in her storytelling that she hadn't realized how long she'd been talking without taking a break.

"There is still much to tell, but I need to rest for a few moments," Singing Bird said as she sat down on the stump behind her, and reached for the water skin.

Sparrow rushed up and handed Singing Bird a small wooden bowl filled with fresh fruit and small cakes.

"You have been speaking for a long time. This should help," she said.

Singing Bird smiled at her as she took the bowl and began to eat. The fruit was sweet and tasty and the cakes were fresh and warm with just a hint of lemon to them.

As she sat there eating and resting, her mind wondered for the hundredth time what went through Silent Runner's mind during this time. She was young and had absolutely no experience as a warrior or of warfare, yet she was making war against a fierce army of yellow haired warriors – and so far, luck and the gods had been on her side.

The food was giving her nourishment and she could feel energy surging back into her insides. There was still more to tell, but soon the story would be finished and she would turn the storytelling over to Sparrow, then await the dark cloud to take her to be with her mother and father and friends.

Singing Bird realized she had shut her eyes and when she opened them, she saw the people sitting quietly, waiting for her to finish telling the story they so cherished. The sun was still shining brightly, but now on the downside of the horizon.

After taking a drink of water from the water skin, Singing Bird stood up and looked out over the people, embedding their smiling faces in her memory. She took a step closer to them, inhaled a deep breath and began.

"Silent Runner and Winter Flower safely guided the people of the clan up the mountain to where the others waited, and when the others saw them approaching, they ran down the short distance to greet them.

"Silent Runner stood off to the side and watched as the clans people crowded around Winter Flower, bombarding her with questions. Silent Runner knew they were questions about her and the animals. She smiled, then walked down through the woods a short distance away, to be alone with her thoughts.

"She had done what she set out to do; rescue her people. But what was she to do now? The Yellow Hairs would be coming for them, of that she had no doubt. And they would be very angry that she had burned their floating things. Her people were not warriors and she had no time to train them before the Yellow Hairs came, she mused.

"According to what Cougar and Wolf had told her, they had captured several other clans. Should she also try to rescue them as well? she wondered.

"Suddenly she began to shiver and tears began to roll down her cheeks. This was turning out to be much more than she'd expected and for the first time she wondered if she had done the right thing by trying to help the people who had turned their backs on both, her and her mother.

"In her heart, they were her people. She had been born into the clan and she couldn't understand why she and her mother had been banished.

"She had been absorbed with her thoughts for some time and hadn't noticed Bear when he sidled up close to her. Feeling his presence, she turned her head and giggled. He was sitting on his haunches, scratching his large stomach.

'What are you doing here?' "she asked."

'I was just wondering why you have water running from your eyes?' "he asked.

"Silent Runner looked at him for a long moment before she replied." 'I'm not sure. I wonder if I'm doing the right thing trying to help people who do not like me.'

"Bear leaned forward and fell back onto all four feet again and padded over closer to her before mind speaking." 'They are human, like you, and therefore, they are your family. We are your friends, but we are animals.'

'But they hate me. Many winters ago, Hawk convinced them to throw my mother and me out of the clan and sent us off to die in the woods,' "Silent Runner said, a defiance in her voice.

"Bear looked at Silent Runner and said," 'They are afraid of you because you were born different from them. They do not yet understand how special you are, but they will when the time comes. The gods have something special in mind for you.'

'Well they'd better hurry up,' "Silent Runner said." 'The Yellow Hairs will be here soon and what am I supposed to do then, draw my sword and fight them all by myself?'

"Cougar and Wolf came walking up to them and Cougar said," 'Have you forgotten our promise to you, already?'

'You are not alone,' "Wolf told her." 'But you need to take your people and leave soon. Your tracks are easy to follow and the Yellow Hairs are on their way here, now.'

'Where shall I take them?' "Silent Runner asked."

'Why not take them to where you and your mother live,' "Bear stated matter-of-factly."

'She can explain everything to them and then maybe they'll understand. After all, some of them already do.'

"Silent Runner looked at her friends and thought, sometimes animals are smarter than humans. How lucky I am to have them as friends.

"Silent Runner's mind went to Winter Flower and the others. They had risked their very lives to come see her and her mother – and had even learned the hand speak language she and her mother had developed.

"She nodded her head and said to Bear with her mind speak," 'You are right. I thank you for your friendship and your advice, for both are good.'

"And with that, she raced back up to the place where the people stood around, listening to Winter Flower and several of the others trying to convince them that Silent Runner and her mother were not possessed by evil demons, but were people just like them.

"She saw Hawk standing to the side, glaring at Winter Flower and the others. She watched as his face turned sullen. He knew he had lost control of the people as their leader and felt he had to do something. He interrupted Winter Flower, telling the people not to be taken in by her lies. He told them Winter Flower and the others were under a spell put on them by Silent Runner and the evil spirits within her."

'Was she not cursed by the gods and banished because of her deformity? Was that not the way it had always been done?' "he asked.

"The people looked from Hawk, to Winter Flower and the women who stood with her, then over to Silent Runner. The confusion they felt showed in their faces.

"Angered by Hawk's stupidity, Silent Runner marched up to him and stood glaring at him. Hawk was surprised by her bravado and wasn't sure what to do, so he glared back at her. He would not be humiliated by this slip of a girl. He was Hawk, leader of the people.

"After a moment, Silent Runner turned to face Winter Flower, and using her hand talk, told Winter Flower to tell Hawk to shut up and stop telling lies. She was only trying to help them - to rescue them from the Yellow Hairs. If they wanted to be used as slaves and whatever else the Yellow Hairs decided to do with them, then they could go back now and she would not stop them. But if they wanted to be free, they would need to open their eyes and see the truth about Hawk, who like the coyote, was cunning, but when faced with danger, slunk away with his tail between his legs.

"Now was not the time to be like the coyote, but time to band together and be strong like the wolf and the cougar and the bear.

"The people began to mumble among themselves and shortly they began to drift over and stand next to Silent Runner, waiting for her to lead them to safety.

"Grinning from ear to ear, Winter Flower made hand talk and told Silent Runner they would follow her. Silent Runner smiled and nodded her head.

"Hawk could see that he was beaten and stepped back, studying Silent Runner. She had grown into a tall, young woman who was doing all the things he wished he had the courage to do. And she did it without lies or cunning. She was brave where he had been weak. And she was somehow able to speak to some of them by making movements of her hands. That, in itself, was a mystery he did not understand. She did not seem evil, nor was what she was doing, evil. She was actually out here, all alone, rescuing the very ones who had turned their backs on her and her mother.

"Had he been wrong about everything? He had been so angry when her mother chose He Who Fishes for a mate instead of him, that he had let his hate fester inside him and when her newborn child could not make any sound, he'd used that to get even with Charlakavos by claiming the baby was cursed. It had been easy to get them banished for he knew the people of the clan believed in ghosts and spirits. But had he done the right thing? Looking at who Silent Runner had become and what she was doing for his people, he suddenly felt ashamed of himself. He began to wonder if he could somehow make it up to her and Charlakavos? If he showed them he had changed, he hoped maybe they would forgive him.

"The people followed as Silent Runner led them away from their temporary hideout.

"She took them up and across the mountain as fast as they could travel. The people looked at her with new eyes because they realized it was Silent Runner, not Hawk, who was the strong one. She had been able to rescue them from the Yellow Hairs because she was not afraid of them, like Hawk, who had advised them to surrender, promising to find a way to escape, later.

"Silent Runner decided the best place to take them would be where she and her mother had been safe these many seasons as Bear had suggested. There was enough room for them, and hidden behind the boulders it would be hard to find. They could stay there safely until she could finish what she'd started. Plus, there were the other clans to try and rescue, if they would come with her.

"She asked for three young men to follow along behind,

wiping out their tracks with leafy branches. At first, they wondered why she would want do this? But after she explained it would make it hard for the Yellow Hairs to follow them, several stepped forward.

"Once again, Hawk marveled at her ingenuity and volunteered to be one of the ones who followed behind, hoping it would be a start.

"Silent Runner looked at Hawk as he ripped a branch from a tree and began brushing out their tracks. Suddenly, there was something different about him but she wasn't sure what it was. He was not being rebellious, which made her wonder what he was up to.

"There was no time to worry about it now. She needed to put as much distance between them and the Yellow Hairs as she could before dark. She also knew they would grumble but there could be no fires tonight to cook with or to keep them warm, but it couldn't be helped. The Yellow Hairs might see the glow of a fire in the night and find them.

CHAPTER NINETEEN

-

"Sven and Lars stood looking at the ground, puzzled by what they saw, or didn't see. The tracks had been plain enough and easy to follow up to now, then all of a sudden, the tracks vanished. It was like they had never been there.

"Sven told several of his men to fan out and search to see it they could find their tracks somewhere off the pathway, but after several minutes they all came back saying the same thing – there were no tracks to be found.

"Lars stood with his hand on his sword, staring into the forest, the hint of fear creeping into his bones, but he fought hard not to let Sven or his men see it."

'Dey did not sprout vings and fly away,' "he said." 'I say vee keep going and see if vee can pick up der tracks farder up da mountain.'

"Without a better idea, Sven agreed with him and ordered the men to follow him and Lars, but to keep a lookout in case they were hiding somewhere off to the side.

"The Yellow Hair warriors did as they were told for they were brave fighting men, but to the man, they were nervous. It was one thing to fight someone you could see and put cold steel into, but spirits were altogether different. They could appear and disappear at will – leave tracks, leading you into danger, then disappear while they waited for you to walk into their trap.

"They had not gone but a short distance when Lars and Sven both raised their arms in the air, bringing the men to an abrupt halt.

"Standing a short distance in front of them were the wild animals Sven had told Lars about. There were mountain lions standing next to giant bears and wolves. They were walking back and forth, snarling and growling with saliva dripping from their jaws. They could see elk shaking their long antlers at them. And the trees ahead were loaded with many different birds of prey, hawks, eagles, crows, as well as others they didn't know the names of."

'Now you see vat I vas talkin' about,' "Sven said in a whisper.

"Lars studied the situation. They looked real enough, but that didn't mean they were.

"Lars stood there, trying to decide what to do. And after just a brief bit of time, he looked at Sven and said," 'I don't believe dey are real. I tink da spirits have conjured dem up ta try and scare us, but I vill not be fooled!'

"And with that, he drew his sword and yelled," 'Attack!'

"The first animal he came to was a huge mountain lion who reached out and swatted the sword from Lars' hand, then leaped on him and knocked him down and suddenly the animals were all around them, growling and snarling - pushing them into a small knot.

"Several of the younger warriors, wanting to exhibit their

bravery, lunged into battle with the animals. Blood was spilled but there were no fatalities on either side, but it was clear the Yellow Hairs were fighting a losing battle against a real enemy, and they had to back off.

"As long as they just stood there, the animals didn't attack. Sven helped Lars to his feet and saw that his hand was bloody where the mountain lion had scratched him.

"Lars glared at Sven," 'He could have killed me, but he didn't. Vhy?'

"Sven looked around, his mind grabbing for answers but they were slow to come." 'I do not know. I tink maybe dey have been told ta keep us here vile da prisoners escape, but not ta harm us.'

'Den dey vould not harm us if vee valked right tru dem?' "Lars asked.

"Again, Sven looked out into the forest and as far as he could see, there were animals."

'I do not know. But vat I do know is, der is more vild animals dan vee can hope ta vade tru. And vee can't push dem aside.'

"They stood there, staring at the animals, who stared back at them. Lars turned and looked back down the trail and saw that it was open."

'Look,' "he said to Sven." 'Dey leave da trail open ta go back da vay vee came.'

'Ya,' "Sven said," 'but for how far? It is getting dark and vee von't be able ta see. Maybe it is a trap. I say vee stay here til morning, den vee can decide vat ta do.'

"Since Lars had no better plan, he made the signal for the men to sit down, which they did, reluctantly, but not before drawing their swords and axes and laying them across their laps. The animals could attack them when they were down on the ground and they could do little to defend themselves. At least with a weapon in their hands they might stand a slight chance.

"The night for the Yellow Hairs turned out to be less than comfortable than for the animals. Early on, black clouds rolled in and then came the rain; falling from the sky like the gods were emptying huge buckets of water on them and all they could do was to sit there and endure it.

"Between the dark clouds overhead, the heavy rain and the thickness of the forest, they couldn't see any farther than a foot or so in front of them."

'Are da animals still out der?' "Lars asked, wiping water from his eyes and face."

'I can't tell,' "Sven said." 'but yer velcome ta get up and go see.'

'No, if anyvon goes ta see it vill be von of da older varriors.'

"And with that he called out," 'Liam, go check and see if da animals are still out der.'

"Liam could barely make out Lars and Sven, let alone, see any animals. He was not a coward and he would follow orders, but that didn't mean he would like it." 'Aye,' "he said as he stood up, looking around nervously. And with his axe in his hand, ready to strike, he ventured toward the darkened forest.

"He hadn't gone far when something batted the axe from his hand and he was rammed in the back by a heavy weight that pushed him forward. He let out a loud scream, which was cut off by something growling loudly in his ear.

"Liam didn't know how far he had been taken into the forest, but was finally deposited next to a large tree and was guarded by a large wolf. In the darkness, he could only make out images, but knew they were all around him and if he moved they would attack and eat him, so he sat quietly and waited, his heart pounding loudly.

"At the sound of the scream, Lars, Sven, and the rest jumped to their feet, swords and axes in their hands, waiting for the attack that never came – just growling and hissing from somewhere beyond their vision."

'It has cost us ah good man, but now vee know,' "Sven said, angrily.

"Not knowing what had actually happened to Liam, he allowed his imagination to run wild, a sadness filling his insides. Liam had been a strong warrior and faithful to him for many years. He hoped for Liam's sake, he had not gone down without a fight.

"Lars stared into the darkness, gritting his teeth. He hadn't wanted Liam killed. At the worst, he figured the old warrior would get growled at, but not killed and maybe eaten."

'I did not tink dey vould actually attack him. I am sorry he is gone. He vas ah good man dat deserved better.'

"After what happened, sitting back down was no longer an option. Cold, hungry and afraid, they stood at the ready, waiting for daylight to come and the storm to pass.

"Just beyond their sight, the animals settled down to wait for morning, knowing they had done their job and Silent Runner and the rest were by now, far up the mountain."

CHAPTER TWENTY

-

"Charlakavos heard them coming and went out to greet them and let out a sigh of relief when she saw her daughter leading the entire clan out of the forest and into the clearing near the entrance to their hideout.

"Silent Runner saw her mother and raced ahead to embrace her, while the rest followed and stood silently, amazed at how well Charlakavos looked and didn't seem to notice her slight limp.

"When they finally stopped hugging each other, Charlakavos smiled at the wide-eyed clans people and said," 'Welcome to our home. You will be safe here until my daughter can finish what she started; and that is to drive the Yellow Hairs far away – back to where they came from, hopefully to never return.'

"The people of the clan suddenly realized they were safe and began to shuffle around, not knowing what to say. The very ones they had shunned were now their protectors.

"To the surprise of everyone, Hawk walked up to the front of the people and looked at Charlakavos and said," 'I think I speak for everyone when I say, thank you for what you and your daughter are doing for us. And personally, I want to say how sorry I am for what I did. I was wrong; I did what I did from anger.'

"He then turned and looked at the people and said," 'I am sorry for not being a good leader. I hope you can forgive me. I should have been the one who was banished for I let my anger control my feelings. I will leave here and never return if that is what you wish.'

"Silent Runner made an instant decision and walked up to him, motioning for her mother to join them.

"With her hand speak, she told her mother what she wanted her to say.

"Charlakavos watched her daughter's hands carefully for she was sure what Silent Runner was saying would be important, and when she'd finished, Charlakavos smiled and turned to Hawk."

'My daughter said to tell you she forgives you and believes she has a way for you to redeem yourself to the people. She wants you and a few braves that you pick, to go with her to drive the Yellow Hairs from our land. She knows it will be dangerous, but if we succeed, then you can stand tall once again.'

"Tears welled up in Hawk's eyes and he had to swallow before he could speak."

'It is more than I deserve and I thank you for the chance to become a new person; one that can walk among his people with his head held high. Yes, I will go with her and give my life if the gods will it.'

"Charlakavos touched him on the arm and whispered," 'You do this and there may be a place next to my fire, after all.'

"Hawk wanted to take her in his arms and hold her near, but

held back. He wanted to make sure he could become the man he hoped he could and then, and only then, could he hope to win her affection.

"Charlakavos herded the people behind the boulders to where they would make their new, temporary home. And as each one passed by the boulders, they made sounds of pleasure and wonder.

"When they were all inside, one of the older women, Charlakavos remembered as, Big Feet, stepped up to her and said," 'I am ashamed of what we did to you and I beg your forgiveness.'

"Charlakavos smiled and hugged her and said," 'Thank you, but there is nothing to forgive. You were influenced by beliefs you thought were right. I can only hope everyone can see now, that most of those beliefs are nothing more than old wives' tales and superstitions passed down from generation to generation.'

"Big Feet stepped back and said," 'Yes, we can see now how foolish we were in our beliefs. It is true; we were led by fear and superstition. I only hope it is not too late to begin over. It will not be easy for it has been our way of life. With your guidance we will try to see the world differently.'

'But we will need a strong leader,' "one of the younger women who had been standing nearby, said." 'How can we change when we don't know what to do? We need someone to show us the way.'

"Charlakavos looked at her and said," 'I believe when the time comes you will all be able to make a wise decision about choosing a new leader.'

"The young woman looked at her, not understanding the implication of her statement, but Big Feet turned her head and watched as Silent Runner, through Winter Flower, went about giving instructions to the men who would go with her to drive the Yellow Hairs from their land, and she nodded her head.

"Hawk and the young men of the clan were overwhelmed by the abilities of the young woman they called, Silent Runner. In every other way except making sounds, she was far superior to them. They had never seen anyone like her and were having difficulty accepting the fact that a woman could do the things she could do, and at such a young age.

"Silent Runner saw this and knew she would need to take things slowly, for everything was new to them and it was hard for them to change, especially when it came to their egos and the way they thought about women.

"She also thought it was funny that these big, so called clan warriors were nothing much more than bravado. They knew nothing about weapons, or fighting other than wrestling. And Hawk seemed to be the only one able to think or plan, but he had always been a schemer.

"She planned to leave at first light tomorrow morning and needed to explain to these young men what their roles would be, and with what turned out to be great insight, she made Hawk her second in command.

"Taking Hawk and Winter Flower aside, she explained her plan to Winter Flower and what she needed for them to do. Then

Winter Flower turned and explained everything to Hawk.

"As Hawk listened, he was relieved to hear they would not be expected to actually fight with the Yellow Hairs, but only to make them think they would. They would be issued axes and other weapons for show, but not expected to use them since they had yet to be trained in the art of warfare."

'I see your logic,' "Hawk said," 'but it will take some doing to get our young braves to walk or stand next to wild animals who have always been our enemies.'

"Silent Runner's hands made their gestures and Winter Flower smiled as she turned to Hawk."

'She said they will not be so afraid when they see you do it first,' "Winter Flower said and watched as Hawk's mouth went slack and he looked like he was about to be sick.

"Hawk swallowed the lump that formed in his throat. The thought of standing next to a wolf or a cougar like they were friends was terrifying and he felt his heart pounding heavily in his chest, praying he would be able to do such a thing.

"After taking several large gulps of air to calm his nerves, Hawk summoned courage from deep inside him and nodded his head, yes. He had to prove not only to himself his courage and loyalty, but to the others as well. It was the only way to become the man he wanted to be. Besides, if Silent Runner could do it, surely it would be all right.

"Silent Runner looked at the sky and knew she had time before it got dark to go over her plan with the young men who had volunteered to go with her. And when, through Hawk, it was explained, she saw real panic in several of their faces."

'You cannot ask us to do this,' "one of the young warriors said."

'If you are afraid, then you can stay here and protect the women,' "Hawk said with as much bravado in his voice as he could muster."

'You are not afraid to do this?' "the young warrior asked of Hawk.

"With courage he didn't really feel, Hawk snickered and said," 'I am Hawk and not afraid of anything. If Silent Runner tells me they will not attack us or eat us, then I believe her.'

'If we see you go among them without fear, then we will go, too,' "another of the young warriors said."

'Then be prepared to go among them tomorrow,' "Hawk said with more confidence than he felt.

"After they had eaten and settled down for the night, Silent Runner and her mother walked out beyond the boulders and looked at a sky filled with brilliant stars and a full moon."

'Will you also try to rescue the other clans who have been taken prisoner?' "Charlakavos asked.

"Silent Runner studied the stars for some time before her hands began to speak." 'It will be my hope, but I do not know if they will trust me. After all, I am no more than a young girl who runs with wild animals. Maybe they will think I am bewitched and be afraid, as did the people of our clan.'

"Charlakavos looked into the eyes of her daughter." 'The gods have given you these gifts for a reason. You may not understand them yet, but I think I do. Yes, you are young and yes, you are a female, but do not let either of these things worry you. When the time comes, you will know what to do.'

"Silent Runner reached out and hugged her mother, hoping she was right. In just a few hours, she would find out.

CHAPTER TWENTY-ONE

-

"As the sun crept over the tops of the trees, Sven, Lars and the rest of their men stood wearily, back to back, weapons in their hands, staring at the woods.

"As the sun rays found their way into the hidden parts of the forest, Sven and the rest of them found themselves staring at nothing but trees."

'Dey are gone!' "Lars said with astonishment.

"Sven looked all around him, as astonished as Lars and all he could say was," 'Ya.'

'Vell, vat do vee do now? Do vee keep looking for da lost prisoners or go back and load up da vons vee have and leave?' "Lars asked, staring directly at Sven.

"Sven looked down at his feet and shook his head. One part of him wanted to go on up the mountain and try to get back his prisoners, but another part of him told him that it would be foolish to try. Whoever was up there might turn the animals on them again and maybe this time with instructions to attack them. Reluctantly, he knew his only choice was to go back and take what prisoners they still had and leave.

"With that decided, they turned and headed back down the mountain.

"To both, Sven and Lars, this seemed the logical thing to do, but they had not counted on a young female warrior with a different plan.

"As Silent Runner and her small band of warriors were ready to set off down the mountain, Wolf arrived and informed her of the events with the Yellow Hairs. She was not content with the animals leaving and giving the Yellow Hairs the opportunity to go back and had to rethink her strategy."

'What if they get back with enough time to load their prisoners on the big floating thing before we can get there?' "Silent Runner asked of Wolf with her mind speak."

'We did not know you wanted to save the others,' "Wolf came back with." 'They have always been your enemy.'

"Silent Runner had to agree with his analogy, but her mind thought differently." 'But what if we could get them to band together? Would we not be stronger and with a little training, be able to stand up against the Yellow Hairs if they should come again?'

'Yes, it would be better if the wolf and the bear and the cougar and all the other animals were friendly, but I'm afraid that will only happen this one time, and only to help you,' "Wolf said with his mind speak, shaking his head."

'I'm sorry for it would be a good thing,' "Silent Runner said."

'What do you want us to do now?' "Wolf asked, trying to change the subject.

"To say the people were stunned at watching Silent Runner and the giant wolf staring at each other as though they were communicating, would be an understatement.

"There were mutterings going on and those who knew of Silent Runner's ability with the animals were afraid the people would revert back to their old feelings.

"Charlakavos saw and heard them and waved her hands to get their attention, and then tried to explain as best she could of the wonderful ability the gods had bestowed on her daughter."

'The gods have chosen her to be special, not deformed as you believed when she was born. Not only did they give her special powers, but wisdom far beyond ours. Even she does not understand what a special person she is. For her, she just wants to be one of us – accepted by you as one of the clan. Please do not judge her until you know and understand more about her.'

"The people could see the wisdom in what Charlakavos said and began to nod their heads. They were slow to come around, but change was hard.

"The people stood silently as they watched Silent Runner, Hawk and the others leave their place of hiding and disappear into the forest; not really understanding what they were going to do other than drive the Yellow Hairs away; each hoping they would return safe."

By now, the sky had turned dark and lanterns had been lit. Singing Bird looked down and saw a young girl holding a wooden bowl in her direction. It was filled with honey cakes, fruit and a large piece of meat, which caused Singing Bird's stomach to grumble.

Smiling at the subtle way she was being asked to take a break and eat something, she reached out and took the bowl, then sat down on the stump of log provided for her and began to eat with relish. She hadn't realized how hungry she was and this would be the final meal she would share with her people. The story would be coming to the end soon, and her time here would be at an end – the dark cloud would be waiting for her.

She chewed the meat slowly, savoring the sweetness of the honey cakes and the bright red strawberries that filled the bowl. She hoped her mother would be there with honey cakes and strawberries when she arrived in the other world.

After finishing her meal and taking a drink from the recently filled water skin, she stood up once again and looked out over the valley. It was time to finish her story.

"Thank you for the delicious meat, honey cakes and strawberries," she said. "Now I must finish the story of our beginning for it is getting late and my time is near."

The people looked back at her and all but the young ones understood her meaning. She was one of the oldest people in the tribe. They would hate to see her go, but that was the way of life. She would be missed, but never forgotten, and as she began to speak they all sat up a little straighter.

"Silent Runner and her small band of warriors moved down the mountain as fast as they dared to go, hoping they would be in time to save the other prisoners, however many of them there may be.

"Sven and Lars sighed a large sigh of relief when they marched out onto the beach and saw their prisoners were still there.

"When the guards saw Sven and Lars, they turned as one and saluted by crossing their arm to their chests.

"Sven strode up to the first guard and said," 'Vee must load dese prisoners onta da ship, now.'

"The guard saluted, again, and turned to the other guards." 'Get da long boats ready, and begin loading da prisoners, and be quick about it.'

"Sven turned and looked at Lars." 'At least vee von't go home empty handed.'

'But ya did lose two ships,' "Lars said with a smirk.

"The implication was not lost on Sven, but he decided to let it pass. After all, this was his last voyage and he could care less if Lars had trouble acquisitioning ships when he was ready to come back. His home overlooking the sea was paid for. He had funds put away that would allow him to live comfortably for the rest of his days. He had only one regret and that was letting that slave woman escape all those years ago. She was so young and beautiful and he would have made her one of his wives. She would have him strong, healthy sons. He was standing, looking at the sky, reminiscing, wondering what happened to her when Lars interrupted him."

'Do not move too quickly, but look around ya.'

"Sven turned slowly and looked around, his teeth mashing together. The wild animals had somehow surrounded them again without them noticing until it was too late. They were even spread across the beach, barring their way to the long boats and their ship."

'So... Vat do vee do now, Sven?' "Lars asked with a sneer."

'It vould seem vee have no choice but ta fight,' "Sven said, signaling for the warriors to come together and form a circle."

'Vee vill move toward da vater and our boats and if dey do not let us tru, vee vill fight our way ta da vater. I vill swim if I have ta, but I vill get out ta da ship and leave dis god forsaken place!' "Sven said, drawing his sword.

"Lars looked at Sven and nodded his head, drawing his own sword. This was something he understood. He was not prepared to die yet, but if it was his time he would go down with a weapon in his hand and a trail of dead animals left behind.

"Sven was about to give the signal to begin moving toward the beach when a young woman dressed as a warrior walked out of the forest and stared at them – her hands on her hips. Behind her stood an older man and ten young men who carried spears.

"Sven recognized the older man and the young warriors. They had been some of the prisoners that escaped. The girl he did not recognize, but there was something about her that disturbed him; something familiar, but he wasn't sure, what it was."

'Vell, if dat von ain't yer spittin' image I'll be cursed,' "Lars said, looking directly at Sven." 'If I didn't know better, I vould svear she vas yer daughter.'

"Sven's mind went instantly to the slave woman who had made her escape, possibly carrying his child. Could this be? he wondered. She looked to be about the right age and he had to admit, she did resemble him in the face. But, ah warrior? Women were not warriors, not even in his own land.

"At this new turn, Sven wasn't sure how to deal with it and Lars saw it in his face."

'Again, vat are vee gonna do now? Ya are da leader and it is up ta ya ta decide, do vee fight, or do vee cringe like small children and give up like da heathen prisoners vee captured? Are ya afraid of a young voman yust because she looks like ya?'

"Sven could see that Lars was ready to go down fighting as was their way and so was he, except, he could not get the young woman out of his mind.

"Taking a deep breath, Sven said," 'Vee vill see vat she vants.'

"And with that, he stepped forward and began to walk toward her until she held up her hand, palm forward, indicating for him to stop. And when he did, she pointed at his hand motioning for him to drop his sword.

"For Sven to give up his weapon was almost more than he could endure. Warriors did not give up their weapons. Showing defiance to her gesture, he replaced his sword into the sheath hanging at his side, then stood staring at her. When she didn't say anything, he looked at Hawk, his eyes blazing daggers, and asked," 'Vat do ya vant?'

"Hawk looked at Silent Runner and when she nodded her head, he said," 'You are free to go aboard your floating thing and go back to where you came from, but you must leave your prisoners with us.'

"From the description her mother had given her, Silent Runner knew without a doubt, this was her father she was facing and she wasn't sure how to deal with it. One part of her wanted to go to him and tell him she was his daughter, to let him see how well she had grown, but the other side of her said, no. She must do what she came here to do – and that was to rescue the prisoners.

"Sven looked at the young female warrior standing bravely in front of him and he also knew he was looking at his daughter. She was beautiful, like her mother, but she also had his eyes and strength. He would love to go to her and tell her who he was and ask her to come home with him, but he knew she would not go. Somehow, she had become the leader of these people, even at her young age and she would not turn her back on them."

'Vell?' "Lars said, breaking his chain of thought.

"How could he tell him he could not go to war against his daughter, yet how could he save face and walk away? Going home without his captives was out of the question, and killing his own daughter was also out of the question. He was perplexed. After taking a large breath of air, he said to Hawk," 'I vill fight yer best varrior and if I vin, ya call off da animals and all of ya vill come vit me as my prisoners.'

"Sven thought this a clever idea, since he saw no one who could best him in a fight and when he won, he would be able to take his daughter home with him without a struggle."

'And if we win?' "Hawk countered."

'Vee leave and ya can have da prisoners as ya asked for earlier,' "he said, never believing this was something that could happen.

"Hawk knew he could not fight this warrior who had scars from many battles and was twice his size. He would not stand a chance. But who else was there? Not one of the young warriors and surely not Silent Runner. She may be able to talk with animals and run very fast, but she was nothing more than a slip of a girl barely into womanhood. His shoulders slumped as he looked over his shoulder at Silent Runner, who to his surprise, stepped forward and pointed her finger at herself."

'No, you cannot fight this man; he is a warrior of many battles. You do not stand a chance,' "Hawk said.

"Silent Runner smiled at Hawk and waved him back to the others, then brushed past him to stand facing her father. She took off all her weapons and indicated with her hands that they would wrestle, which Winter Flower interpreted to Sven and the others."

'Vat's da matter, can she not speak fer herself?' "Sven asked.

"Hawk stepped back up next to her and said," 'No, she was born without the ability to make sounds, so she speaks with her hands.'

'Vat kind of sorcery is dis?' "Lars shouted."

'I promise you, it is not sorcery. She is just like anyone else in every other way.' "he said, omitting the part where she ran with and communicated with the wild animals.

"Sven did not want to fight his daughter, not even wrestle her, which he knew he was much superior at. Was he not the wrestling champion of their village? In fact, he was champion in all the sports. It had been years since anyone had bested him at anything."

'Ya da not expect me ta wrestle vit dis slip of a girl? I vould break her in two, yust like dat,' "he said, snapping his fingers.

"Silent Runner raised her hand to her mouth as though she was stifling a yawn, which caused even the prisoners to laugh."

'She does not seem ta be afraid of da champion vrestler of Hogshead,' "Lars said with a bit of a smirk." 'Maybe ya should tell her. Maybe den she vill not vant ta vresle vit ya.'

"It was more than Sven could take. He would not be laughed at, especially not by the prisoners.

"Without a word, he took off his helmet, his sword, his boots, and threw down his shield, then stepped off to the side and opened his arms."

'Ven ebber ya are ready,' "he said, testily, wanting to get this over with.

"Silent Runner looked at her father and sighed. He was not only big, like the bears she had wrestled with as she had grown up, but he had hands to grab her with, and if he ever got a hold on her, she would be finished. She knew she would not be able to break his hold on her – he was too big and strong. She would need to stay away from him and use some of the tricks she had made up when battling the animals. She did not know if they would work on humans, but she had to try, it was the only way she would have a chance to win.

"She began to circle him, watching his every move and saw

that he was quick, and he was watching her too."

'Are vee gonna vrestle or are vee gonna dance da circle all day?' "he asked, trying to get her to come within his grasp.

"But Silent Runner did not fall for his trap. Instead, she began to move back and forth, darting in and out, causing him to reach for her and slipping away before he could grab her in his large, muscular hands. His eyes and facial expression told Silent Runner it would not be long before he would get tired of this and charge her, which is exactly what she wanted him to do.

"She had just darted in toward him when he rushed to meet her, his arms reaching out to grab her and pull her to him.

"But she saw him coming and being younger and faster, she ducked under his tree like arms and circled around behind him and raised her foot and planted it squarely on his rear end and shoved as hard as she could.

"Moving forward and already off balance, Sven was sent sprawling face first onto the sand, which raised a great cloud of dust.

"Getting to his feet and spitting sand from his mouth, he glared at his daughter. Over her shoulder, he could see the prisoners staring at them, some with their hands over their mouths, stifling a laugh.

"Sven roared," 'so dat is how vee are gonna play da game. So be it, now it is no longer vrestling, but no holds barred bare handed fightin'.'

"And with that, Sven bent over at the waist and with his arms spread wide, and charged her like a raging bull.

"Silent Runner watched him come and gauged her timing. Just as he came within arms reach, she leaped in the air, causing him to run under her, his arms grabbing nothing but air.

"She had gauged his movement right and came down with both feet against his back, kicking him with both feet, then leaped to the side as Sven went head first into the sand, again, and this time heard their laughter.

"As Sven came to his feet, he was both embarrassed and raging mad. To be made sport of by this slip of a girl was more than his ego could stand. While another side of him was bursting with pride that his daughter was holding her own against him, but this side he could not show."

'Sven, do ya vant me ta send von of my men ta help ya? This wee slip of a girl has put ya face down in da sand twice now, and has yet ta lay ah hand on ya,' "Lars yelled out.

"Sven turned and glared at Lars." 'As I recall, I have beat ya ever time vee vrestled, so I don't need none of yer mouth. If ya tink ya can do better, come and take my place.'

"Lars spat into the sand and said nothing, then motioned with his hand for Sven to continue.

"Sven looked at his daughter and approached her with more caution this time; moving toward her slowly, his hands out in front of him, waiting for the opportunity to grab her and get this over with.

"Silent Runner watched him come, trying to figure his next move. She watched his eyes, which she had learned, were a give away to what he was about to do.

"They were no more than two feet apart when she saw his eyes go wide and knew he was about to lunge. She waited and when he did, she stepped toward him and with one hand, grabbed him by his beard and yanked, while throwing her shoulder into his stomach area and lifting with her other hand.

"His weight almost buckled her knees, but she shoved upward with her legs and felt him go into the air, doing a somersault, then landing flat of his back with a loud whoosh of air coming from his mouth.

"Sven lay there for a moment, trying to regain the breath that had been knocked out of him, wondering where she had learned to do that. His body ached but he was not done yet and climbed to his feet and motioned for them to continue.

"Silent Runner looked at her father and felt pride in the fact that he had not given up, but she was also afraid. He was a much more experienced fighter than she was – this being her first fight with another human being.

"Sven moved toward her, his eyes watching her carefully as she began to back away, trying to stay just out of his reach. She was so intent on watching him she did not see the large piece of driftwood behind her and tripped over it before Hawk could warn her.

"Silent Runner went down hard and had the wind knocked out of her and before she could get back to her feet, she felt Sven grab one of her ankles and begin to drag her down the beach so the others could see him destroy her.

"She kicked with her other foot and jerked her leg but his grip was too strong."

'Now it vill be over,' "Sven said to Lars and the rest of the Yellow Hairs standing on the beach.

"Still holding on to her ankle, Sven reached down and grabbed Silent Runner by the hair of her head. Daughter or no, she had humiliated him in front of Lars and his men and this he would not tolerate.

"Letting go of her ankle, he wrapped his arms around her and began to squeeze as he leaned his mouth close to her ear."

'I know ya are my daughter and ya have fought vell. I am proud of ya, but daughter or no, ya have made me look veak in front of my men and for dat I cannot show mercy. I am sorry my daughter but ya must die; dey vill demand it.'

"For a full second, Silent Runner thought she was about to die, but something inside her told her to fight!

"She could feel his arms tightening against her chest, driving the air from her lungs and knew she had to do something fast or she would die.

"Silent Runner twisted her body just enough to relieve some of the pressure and then opened her mouth and bit Sven on the arm as hard as she could.

"Sven let out a yell, but his grip on her was only lessened a small amount, but that had to be enough, she thought, as she wiggled loose from his grip and stepped away just far enough to reach down and grab a hand full of sand, which she tossed into his eyes, then moved away, trying to decide what to do next.

"Sven grabbed at his eyes, trying to wipe the sand from them, which only made it worse. Half blind he reached for her and stumbled.

"He fell, head first, his forehead striking a rock protruding from the beach. They heard a loud snap when his neck broke.

"Suddenly everything was quiet except for the small waves lapping the shore.

"Silent Runner stood, looking down at her father. She had not wanted to harm him. She only wanted him and the other Yellow Hairs to leave and not come back. What was she going to tell her mother? she wondered. She could feel the tears welling up in her eyes and blinked, trying to hold them back."

'So, ya haft beaten Sven, but dat does not mean ya are free ta take my prisoners. No. All of ya are now my prisoners and if ya do not vish ta die, ya vill tell yer people ta go ta da ship quietly,' "Lars said, brandishing his sword."

'But you said...' "Hawk yelled."

'I said nuthin,' "Lars said with a no nonsense tone to his voice." 'Ya ver dealin' vit Sven, but as ya can see, Sven can no longer speak fer himself. So now I, Lars, am in charge and ya are all my prisoners,' "he said, waving his arm around to encompass both Silent Runner's small group and the large group of prisoners standing nearby.

"Silent Runner had listened to Lars and knew her battle was not over, but also knew he would not consent to a hand to hand combat with her.

"After a moment, she began to make talk with her hands and Winter Flower watched carefully so she would be able to translate Silent Runner's words without any mistakes. When Silent Runner finished, Winter Flower smiled at her friend's courage. She stepped up next to Hawk and whispered in his ear.

"Hawk nodded his head then turned to Lars and said," 'Silent Runner has said she will allow you to leave in peace, and take Sven with you, but the people stay with us.'

"Lars tilted his head back and roared with laughter and when he finished, his eyes were cold as ice and his face showed his anger."

'Ya can tell her; Lars does not take orders from vomen, especially vons who cannot speak fer demselves. Ya can tell her, she can go aboard my ship or she can die, here on dis beach. Da choice is hers.'

'She can understand you,' "Hawk told him."

"Lars turned his glare on Silent Runner and she knew his answer. She sighed, knowing she had no other choice and raised her fingers to her temples and closed her eyes.

"Suddenly growls from bears, roars from cougars, howls from wolves and a lot of other animal sounds filled the air causing Lars and his men to look around them. They watched as the animals came from the forest, walking toward them.

"Lars called his men to him and they formed a circle, facing the animals from all directions – weapons at the ready.

"At the sight of the oncoming ferocious, snarling, growling wild animals, the prisoners huddled together, waiting to be torn to pieces along with the Yellow Hairs, by these howling, snarling wild beasts that had always been their enemy.

"Instead, the animals parted and went around them and moved toward the Yellow Hairs.

"As the animals got close, Silent Runner stepped up close to Hawk and raised her arms, causing the animals to stop less than ten feet from the Yellow Hairs.

"Lars looked toward Silent Runner, but it was Hawk who said," 'She is giving you one last chance to leave peacefully. If you choose to make a fight of it, some of the animals may die, but in the end, they will feast on your flesh.'

"Lars looked out over the sea of wild animals, hunger written on their faces and knew he would help fill their bellies if he didn't heed her warning. There were just too many of them. He was not a fool and knew he could come back with many warriors and get his revenge. So, with great reluctance, and with the thanks of his men, he finally relented to leave peacefully and leave his prisoners behind.

"They stood on the shore and watched as the ship unfurled its sails and began moving toward the open water.

"Once Lars knew he was safe from attack, he stepped on the highest part of the deck and yelled, 'I vill be back and ven I do, I vill not fail!'

CHAPTER TWENTY-TWO

-

"When the ship disappeared beyond the horizon, Silent Runner turned and indicated that they make camp for the night. There were provisions left by the Yellow Hairs so they would have food to eat.

"At first there was reluctance. After all they were from several different clans and each wanted to go their separate ways, but when they noticed the animals were still there and doing her bidding, they were too scared to go against her. Even though she was a female, she was a female with strength and power over wild beasts and had proved herself as a warrior.

"Fires were lit, food prepared and by the time they finished eating, the moon had taken control of the sky. It had been an exhausting day and they were tired. As the fires died down, snoring could be heard throughout the camp.

"The young warriors of Silent Runner's group took turns keeping watch to make sure the Yellow Hairs did not return during the night, nor any of the clans try to sneak away.

"When morning came, Silent Runner gathered them all together and while they ate their breakfast, she told them, through

Winter Flower they had two choices. First, and the one she hoped they chose, was to come with her and join with the others who had already escaped."

'Together we can stand against the Yellow Hairs when they return, which I know they will. Or, you can go back to where you came from and take your chances when they come back.'

"There was much muttering and shaking of heads. Arguments sprung up quickly but without altercations.

"Finally, three men stood up and approached Silent Runner, Winter Flower and Hawk. They had been chosen to speak for the three clans.

"The oldest of the three was tall, with stooped shoulders and had a head as smooth as a sandstone, and a wispy, thin beard. He stepped forward and nodded toward Silent Runner, then turned to Hawk with his questions."

'I am Wild Horse and these two,' "he said indicating the two men standing next to him, who looked to be typical clan leaders," 'are Hunter and Otter Tail, both leaders of their clans. We have counseled and I was chosen to ask the questions. When we have the answers, we will council and then make our decision.'

"Hawk looked at Silent Runner who nodded her head.

'Ask your questions,' "Hawk said to him."

'First, who is this girl to be giving orders? We have never taken orders from women and don't plan on starting now.'

'She has been called by several names. As a newborn, she was called Hummingbird, which is a story to be heard. At birth, she could make no sound and she and her parents were banished from the clan. Then a few seasons later the people saw her running in the forest with mountain lions, bears and even wolves, but we heard no noise, so we changed her name to Silent Runner. If running with wild animals was not strange enough, we found out she can communicate with people by moving her hands and mind talking with animals, as you have seen her do. And as you have also seen, she is a mighty warrior. Who of you could have beaten the Yellow Hair as she did? If there are any of you who want to challenge her for her position, now is the time to come forward,' "Hawk said with pride in his voice."

"When none of them stepped forward, Hawk made a brave statement to cement her as the leader of the group."

'Because of what she has done and who she has become, I give her a new name, one that befits her position. From this day forward she shall be called, Guardian Warrior, for she has risked her own life to set all of us free.' "Looking around he asked," 'Are there any here who can challenge that?'

'But we do not follow females,' "Wild Horse said."

'Then you are free to go your own way. If you come with us, you will follow her. If not, you will deal with the Yellow Hairs without our help when they return. All of you who are leaders of your clan will be sub chiefs, but Guardian Warrior will be our supreme leader,' "Hawk said with conviction.

"Silent Runner or Guardian Warrior, or whatever they planned to call her now stood in awe of what Hawk was saying. She was stunned. Supreme leader?

"It was Winter Flower who, with her hands moving very swiftly said," 'Finally, you have been given the title you deserve. I am so proud and honored to be your friend and I will follow you wherever you lead us.'

"Silent Runner sighed and then began to move her hands." 'I do not want to be a leader. I have seen only fourteen summers. I have just barely come into womanhood – and I am a female. Besides, I'm not sure I would even know how. No, tell them I do not want to be their leader. There has never been a female leader.'

'Then you will be the first,' "Winter Flower pronounced, paying no attention to her refusal to be their leader."

'What do they say?' "Wild Horse asked, indicating Silent Runner and Winter Flower.

"Hawk shook his head and said," 'I do not know for I have not yet learned to do the hand speak.'

'Then how are we supposed to follow this, this, this, slip of a female when we cannot communicate with her?' "Wild Horse bellowed – his two companions nodding their heads in agreement.

"Hawk looked to Winter Flower for help and she grinned, happy to be included."

'It is not hard to learn and until everyone can hand speak, there will be those of us who can, will translate her words until you learn,' "Winter Flower said with authority."

'But, but...' "was all Wild Horse could say before Silent Runner stepped in front of him and looked him in the eyes, then moved her hand and pointed at herself, then placed her palm across her mouth to indicate silence, and then with two fingers made a sign of running.

"Wild Horse looked at her and grinned when he understood she was telling him her name. And when she pointed at him, he said," 'I am called Wild Horse.'

"Silent Runner shook her head no, and pointed at his hands.

"He nodded and thought for a moment, wondering how he could make her understand his name. Then out of the blue it came to him and he waved his hands and arms in the air and jumped around like a wild person, then moved his arms and legs like a horse running.

"Silent Runner grinned and drew a picture of a horse running in the sand and pointed to him. Wild Horse shook his head yes.

"It took them no more time to come to a decision than it took for Silent Runner to take a drink from the water skin she carried.

"Wild Horse walked up to Hawk and asked," 'You are sub chief of this one you call Guardian Warrior?'

"Hawk looked at Silent Runner and she grinned and nodded her head, yes, knowing at this point she had no other choice.

"Filled with pride, Hawk turned back to Wild Horse and said," 'Yes, I am sub chief to Guardian Warrior. What is your decision?'

"Wild Horse looked at his two companions, who nodded their heads. He looked back at Hawk and said, 'We will follow her, for now, but she still must prove herself to be a strong leader.'

CHAPTER TWENTY-THREE

-

"The two-day trip back up the mountain was hard because it rained the entire way and caused many problems, such as finding a sheltered place to rest at night, and dry wood for their fires.

"They were all soaked to the skin by the time the sun went down and the temperature had dropped, leaving them shivering and cold. Many complained and wondered when they would get where they were going.

"The morning of the third day came with sunshine and warmer weather, which helped everyone's mood. And after a word from Winter Flower, Hawk announced they would be at their new camp in time for the noonday meal, which brought about cheers.

"One of the young warriors who had been standing guard ran up to Charlakavos and announced a large group of people were coming up the mountain and they were not Yellow Hairs.

"Charlakavos ran out and stood in front of the boulders, staring into the forest, her excitement building by the minute, and when she saw her daughter at the head of the people, she ran to meet her.

"Hawk and the others watched as they embraced, then followed them into the camp, where each clan separated into small groups, still unsure of what to do.

"Silent Runner told her mother of what Hawk had said and done and when they looked around they caught a glimpse of him disappearing into the forest, carrying a long spear.

Silent Runner started to go after him to see where he was going, but a small skirmish broke out between two of the young men; one from Silent Runner's clan and the other from one of the new clans that had just arrived.

"Silent Runner stepped in between them and pushed them apart, shaking her head, no. With her hand speak she told Winter Flower what to say.

"Winter Flower watched to make sure she got the message correct and then turned to the two young men."

'We do not make war with each other. If we are to stand against the Yellow Hairs, we must do it as one. If you cannot get along, then both of you will be turned out.'

"The two young men looked at each other, then one of them reached out his hand and they grabbed wrists.

"Silent Runner turned and looked at the three clans, all separate from each other and sighed. These people had lived as enemies for so long, she was not sure she could bring them together as one clan."

Singing Bird stopped and reached down and picked up her water skin. It had been awhile since she'd had a drink and her throat was feeling the effects. Taking her time, she let the cool water trickle down her throat and felt its soothing effect. And when she felt strength oozing into her again, she turned back to the people sitting in front of her and resumed. The story was almost to its end and she could finish it now.

"For two days, Silent Runner, or Guardian Warrior as she was mostly called now, settled disputes among the three clans; each wanting something the others didn't.

"On the afternoon of the second day, Hawk came walking into camp with a deer across his shoulders. He walked up to Charlakavos and lifted the deer off his shoulders and laid it at her feet.

"Everyone stopped what they were doing and watched, for in all the clans, this meant the same, Hawk was proclaiming his love for Charlakavos and asking her to accept him as her mate, promising to provide for her.

"Charlakavos looked at her daughter and saw tears in her eyes and both hands held tightly against her chest, right over her heart.

"Charlakavos turned and looked at Hawk, who stood nervously awaiting her answer. According to what Silent Runner and everyone else had said, Hawk had changed and had even been made second in command by her daughter.

"After a long moment, Charlakavos smiled and nodded her head in agreement.

"There was much excitement and all three clans forgot their disagreements, at least long enough to plan a wedding ceremony and the party that would follow.

"A medicine man from one of the clans offered, as a token of friendship, to perform the ceremony and seeing this as a way of pulling them together, he was given the nod.

"Wedding ceremonies were normally short and to the point; the taking of hands and agreeing to mate for life, but not this time. The old medicine man, who was tall and as of late had not been much in need, spoke of the hard times they were going through and of this new chance they'd been given. He even alluded to this wedding as a sign of good things to come; and then finally after what seemed to be a long time, pronounced them mates for life.

"From somewhere, drums magically appeared and two men had flutes. Music flowed, people danced and cheered as Hawk and Charlakavos sneaked off into the woods.

"A few days later, Silent Runner – Guardian Warrior, was instilled as the leader of the new clan now to be called, a tribe, and was to be named, Che-O-Wa Nation; which meant, Strength as One.

"Over the next few weeks Silent Runner – Guardian Warrior spent time writing down a set of rules for them to live by. One, all people would respect one another. Two, all people, both male and female had a say in all laws. Three, all leaders were to be elected by the people and if they did not do a good job, they could be challenged and a vote taken to see if they stayed or were replaced.

"The rules went on to cover as many aspects of their lives as she could think of and asked questions of people from all three clans.

"There would be classes on warfare and on weapons. Wanton killing of animals was prohibited and hunting could only be done as needed to survive. And when an animal was killed, thanks were to be given to the gods for providing for them and also to the animal for sacrificing his or her life."

Singing Bird took a breath and looked out over the people, before finishing her story.

"Silent Runner – Guardian Warrior was a good leader, but because of her strength and wisdom, no males approached her until several years later. A warrior who was called, Raging Water because his fighting skills were as strong as a raging river, came to her one day and laid a deer at her feet.

"Her mating celebration lasted seven days, which was the longest of any that could be remembered.

"Over the next several years, the Yellow Hairs came and each time they were repelled because we stood as one," Singing Bird said with pride.

"Over the years we grew to be the people we are today because of her courage and teaching. Silent Runner will be remembered as the one who gave life to the great Che-O-Wa Nation, and I am proud to be one of her descendents," Singing Bird said with a smile.

"Always remember we are who we are because of the courage of a young woman who never gave up on her dream."

The people stood and cheered as Singing Bird bowed her head.

Sparrow came up next to her and started to drape a large skin over her shoulders, but she shook her head, no.

Sparrow helped Singing Bird to her hut where she changed into a long, white buckskin dress with several colors of beads sewn in a beautiful pattern. Sparrow combed and entwined feathers in Singing Bird's hair, allowing it to hang down her back.

Feeling beautiful and almost youthful again, Singing Bird said she was ready and they went outside, to be greeted by the entire tribe. They were waiting for her and walked with her to the edge of the forest, singing songs of her praise.

They stood in awe as Singing Bird walked regally toward the waiting black cloud. And as she neared, the cloud opened. Thunder roared and lightning lit up the night.

Suddenly, standing next to Singing Bird was an old woman with wrinkled skin and long white hair. She locked her arm into Singing Bird's arm and they walked together toward the light and when they got close, Singing Bird could see her mother and father, and all her friends who had gone on before her, waiting with outstretched arms.

Singing Bird turned back one last time and waved to the people of the tribe, then swung around and with Silent Runner – Guardian Warrior by her side, walked into the arms of her mother and father.

Sparrow watched as the black cloud closed in around them and knew there would be a new ending to the story.

THE END

FROM THE AUTHOR

Thank you for your readership. And remember, writers need your reviews, whether they be long or short.

MEET THE AUTHOR

At the current time, Jared McVay lives in the great northwest, where he writes his stories and does storytelling. Many consider him a Master Storyteller. Jared is also a three-time award-winning author. He writes several genres, which includes - westerns, fantasy, and action/adventure. But mainly, he writes about people and their struggles with everyday life.

Before becoming an author, he was a professional actor – on stage, in movies and television. As a young man he was a cowboy, a rodeo clown, a lumberjack, a power lineman, a world-class sailor and spent his military time with the Navy Sea Bees where he learned his electrical trade.

When not writing, you can find him fishing somewhere, or traveling around and just enjoying life with his girlfriend, Jerri.

THANK YOU
FOR READING!

If you enjoyed this book, we would appreciate your customer review on your book seller's website or on Goodreads.

Also, we would like for you to know that you can find more great books like this one at www.CreativeTexts.com

  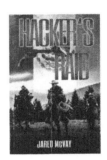

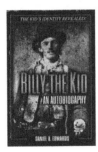  

71769428R00121